BLACK SHEET VENGEANCE

BLACK SHEET
VENGEANCE

HARRY BROOKS CRAYTON

Copyright © 2019 by Harry Brooks Crayton.

Library of Congress Control Number:		2019903836
ISBN:	Hardcover	978-1-7960-2504-0
	Softcover	978-1-7960-2503-3
	eBook	978-1-7960-2502-6

All rights reserved. No part of this book may be reproduced or transmitted in any form or by any means, electronic or mechanical, including photocopying, recording, or by any information storage and retrieval system, without permission in writing from the copyright owner.

This is a work of fiction. All of the characters, names, incidents, organizations, and dialogue in this novel are either the products of the author's imagination or are used fictitiously.

Any people depicted in stock imagery provided by Getty Images are models, and such images are being used for illustrative purposes only.
Certain stock imagery © Getty Images.

Print information available on the last page.

Rev. date: 04/01/2019

To order additional copies of this book, contact:
Xlibris
1-888-795-4274
www.Xlibris.com
Orders@Xlibris.com

CONTENTS

Chapter 1 1
Chapter 2 12
Chapter 3 Homecoming..35
Chapter 4 Home At Last 58
Chapter 5 My House At Last 70
Chapter 6 Steve Grayson 86
Chapter 7 Oceans Looks Around 108
Chapter 8 Sniper Attack 138
Chapter 9 The Dance 152

Acknowledgments 181

To my wife, Deborah, who gave me the encouragement and space to write this book

My love and my thanks

If you enjoyed the book *Black Klansman* and its subsequent movie, you will love Black Sheet Vengeance.

BLACK SHEET VENGEANCE

By Harry Brooks Crayton

MISSION: CREATE DISTRUST FOR AND AMONG THE KKK IN CALOOSA AND DISCOURAGE THEM FROM TERRORIZING COLORED PEOPLE!

Oceans is a boy growing up in the fictitious town of Caloosa, Mississippi, in the 1920s and 1930s under the Jim Crow system and Ku Klux Klan dominance. He sees his mentor and other colored men face injustice from the system and lynchings by the Klan and determines that one day, he will rid his town of the Klan menace. Somehow he will find a way to terrorize individual members of the Klan and make them scared to wear the white sheet and hood, much less terrorize the colored population. As a young army volunteer in World War ll, he faces all types of discrimination. The colored GIs are segregated as well as undervalued, underestimated, and marginalized. He is assigned as a truck driver even though his testing shows that he is qualified for much more. His truck is blown up, and he is captured by the Germans and sent to a prison camp where he escapes and ends up fighting with the French underground.

He returns home after the war to use his skills with weapons and his God-given ability to mimic any voice or accent once he's heard it to rescue colored men from lynchings by the Klan by disguising himself as a white man and eventually terrorizing the Klan to the point that they're afraid to show themselves.

CHAPTER 1

They caught him coming out of the white-only toilet at the Texaco Gas Station buttoning up his overalls, but this wasn't the first Jim Crow law Osei Obiri Blackman had broken. He was a regular repeat offender when it came to breaking Mississippi laws. Mississippi had so many laws for the colored citizens that it was impossible not to break one even if you tried, and Obiri didn't even try. In fact, he went out of his way to break as many of these unjust laws as he could. He was defiant, rebellious, and determined to relentlessly challenge these restrictive, unfair, and discriminatory laws even though it was to his own detriment. He had said many times that he was willing to die for his beliefs. In his opinion, the disparagement between black and white in Mississippi in the 1940s left blacks not much better off than the years immediately following the Civil War. They were not slaves but not totally free either. According to Osei Obiri, colored people were at the low end of a caste system and had no power to determine their own future. In addition to the bias and restrictive Jim Crow laws, the Ku Klux Klan ran rampant in colored neighborhoods, burning, shooting, and lynching at will.

There was colored freedom and white freedom. Colored freedom was defined by a Jim Crow system, which was introduced shortly after the Civil War reconstruction period. These Jim Crow laws promised to guarantee separate but equal treatment. But the only part of the guarantee colored folks got was the separate. Turns out the white definition for *equal* was inferior treatment and facilities, also lack of access to education, hotels, theaters, restaurants, transportation, and even the military. Voting was denied, and trying to vote was suicide. Hundreds of thousands of colored people were caught in this deadly Jim Crow crunch. They were completely helpless under the staggering weight of these racist laws. A simple act of looking a white person in the eye, drinking from the wrong fountain, not stepping off the sidewalk when approaching a white person, be it man woman or child, or using a white-only toilet could get a colored person lynched. Osei Obiri knew all of this and still challenged these laws every chance he got. He had seen colored men hanged, burned, dragged, castrated, and more for the least little infraction, but that didn't discourage his resistance. Most colored people accepted their fate with little protest and prayed things would get better. Prayer is good Obiri acknowledged, but we need to show our dissatisfaction with action too. He told his wife Asantehemaa Afua, who had retained her African name and given their children African names as well, "We have nothing to look forward to and only white dominance to look back on. The white man has taken everything from us. We can't let him take our roots, our language, and our history. Most of our black neighbors have forgotten or renounced their roots, and those who remember don't want to be identified with it. They're ashamed to be from Africa, the country of their ancestors. They don't realize how important it is to remember their roots. We must continue to remind them."

He stressed, "We share this city with white Irish, English, Italian, and even Germans, and they're all proud of their roots. Why can't we be proud of ours? Even if it kills me, I've got to make our black neighbors see that our hope lies in knowing our past. If I can convince one person, I'll consider that progress."

Osei Obiri was proud of his African lineage and made sure everyone knew it. In his own way, he fought against the injustice of Jim Crow laws. He was defiant, rebellious, and sometimes even reckless.

Colored and white both thought he was strange because he was different. Some thought he was born 200 years too late—a throwback to ancient times. Black folks didn't understand him—they were trying to live in the present. White folks thought his rhetoric was inflammatory and might influence rebellion while colored people saw his rhetoric as just big talk that would lead to conditions getting worse, and many were hostile toward him.

He was the fifteenth generation of his family born in America and could trace his roots back 200 years. His colored neighbors could barely go back two generations. He could speak Akan, the native language of his people, and taught it to his son, Yeboa, and Owusu Ansa, his daughter. Most colored folks didn't even know or care what their native language had been. Every chance he got, he expressed the importance of knowing your roots. He boasted to anyone who would listen that he was named after Ashanti kings.

His ancestors lived in the Golden City of Kumasi in West Africa. His adopted religion was Christian Baptist, but he knew that his ancestors worshiped the Golden Stool, a religious symbol known as the soul of the Ashanti people. According to legend, high priest and magician Okomfo Anokye made the Golden Stool appear and float out of the sky and land on the lap of Osei Tutu, the first Asantehene-Asante king. This symbol united his people. They later became Muslims but still saw the Golden Stool as a religious symbol.

He walked the streets of Caloosa, Mississippi, with his head high. He was a genius at working with wood and metal—a trade passed down through the generations. He was self-sufficient, self-possessed, and proud of his independence, all of which he owed to his ancestors. Not even the racist Jim Crow laws could take that away from him.

Most of his colored neighbors shunned him. They thought that many of their problems were owing to his defiance. Yet they admired his intelligence, independence, and shrewdness. But one of the neighborhood children seemed to gravitate to him. His mother had named him Oceans, which would have made him ostracized too had he not been so strong willed and outgoing. Obiri took him under his wing and became his mentor.

Oceans frequented Obiri's house and was fascinated by the stories Obiri told of the Ashante Empire, Osei Tutu, the first Asantehene king, and Okomfo Anyoke and the Golden Stool all fascinated him. Osei Obiri taught him all he knew about wood- and metalwork and the history of the African people going back over two centuries.

Every day after school, Oceans would abandon his friends for a few hours and go to Osei's shop to learn the intricacies of wood- and metalwork. He was a quick study and learned much in the next few months, including Obiri's love for his heritage. This love was passed on to Oceans. He often told his father, "He treats me like one of his children."

"The white man will try to keep you out of his schools of higher learning," Obiri told Oceans, "but this trade he can never take away from you. Learn it well, and you will never have to depend on his charity. Learn as much as you can now because I won't be here to teach you later."

"Are you going north too?" Oceans asked innocently. He knew that many colored families were migrating north to get away from the restrictions of Jim Crow.

"I'll be dead before too many months have passed," Obiri answered honestly. "Remember what I have taught you and use it for the benefit of your family and my family."

Osei Obiri had shown no regret (emotion) after being caught using the white bathroom. "It was my right as a citizen of Caloosa," he calmly explained. "You go look in that stinking pigpen and see if you can tell my pee from the rest. I wasn't going to pee in my pants because a sign said 'white only.' Pee is pee."

Wesley Simmons, the grand dragon of the KKK and the most narrow-minded, bigoted, and warped racist in Caloosa arrived just in time to hear Obiri explaining. "You've broken every law we have, nigger," Wesley growled. "This time you're going to pay."

"You try living by those humiliating regulations white folks dreamed up for us Negroes. Your controlling laws are just as bigoted as you are, you pompous-ass peckerwood," Obiri snapped. "You're like an evil spirit dragged up from the deepest part of hell."

A few Negroes were standing nearby witnessing the spectacle and could barely control the pride and admiration they felt for this man whom they had ostracized for so long simply because of his resistance to the Jim Crow laws that kept them all in virtual slavery.

"Don't sass me, nigger."

"How can one man sass another?" Obiri challenged.

"You may think you special with your African name and your African roots, but you just another nigger," the grand dragon declared. "And don't you dare look me in the eye when I'm talking to you, you hear."

Obiri was not easily intimidated. "You may think you're special because you're white, Mr. Grand Dragon." Obiri spat out. "But you're nothing but trash, and once more, I think you know it."

While he was saying this, Obiri was jabbing his finger into the grand dragon's chest, making him back up. Obiri thought it was almost comical the way the grand dragon was huffing and puffing and making animated hand gestures and facial expressions trying to think of a retort to this surprising confrontation. Deeply offended and losing face in front of the white onlookers, he had to do something. Unable to come up with a verbal response, the grand dragon then slapped him and, to his and the crowd's surprise, quickly received an unexpected return slap, but Obiri didn't stop with a slap. He threw a vicious fist to the grand dragon's face. Before anyone could intervene, Osei Obiri had hit that white arrogant face until it turned from pompous and uppity to fear, panic, shame, and confusion. All the time, Osei Obiri was looking him in his eyes with a lopsided grin on his face. He knew he had signed his death warrant but didn't care. He just kept swinging until someone started beating him in the back of the head.

The sheriff had arrived by then, and Osei Obiri Blackman was hammered into unconsciousness with nightsticks by the sheriff and his deputies.

"Lynch the nigger!" someone yelled from the crowd.

"No! No!" the grand dragon screamed, raising his hand to stop the crowd. "I want him to be fully awake. Put him in jail. Let him worry about it a few days."

Wesley Simmons didn't look much like a respected grand dragon of the KKK—he was bleeding from the mouth, nose, and ears. In the short time before the sheriff intervened, he had taken a brutal and vicious beating.

Osei Obiri was neither foolish nor naïve. He knew that he was fighting a good cause and that it would cost him his life. He only hoped that his message was received, and he wasn't dying in vain. He had tried unsuccessfully to remake his people in his own image. He only hoped his death would succeed in opening someone's eyes.

Hester and Enoch, the only real friends the Blackmans had, and their son, Oceans, had practically adopted the Blackman twins even though they were much younger.

Osei Obiri sat in his jail cell, pondering his fate and wondering how long he had to wait before facing a Ku Klux Klan lynch mob when he heard a voice whispering his name through the jail window. To his surprise, it was sixteen-year-old Oceans Tires. "What in the world are you doing here, Oceans? You should be in school. Don't you know it's dangerous coming around here?"

"I just want to help."

"Then don't get yourself killed. Remember what I've taught you. You're a smart boy, and one day you'll find a way to fight the injustice that colored people have to face, but you're not ready yet. Just remember, watch out for Wesley Simmons. He's dangerous to Negro progress. His hate has no bounds. Tell my family I said goodbye and I love them. Remember me and take care of each other. Now get out of here before you get caught."

After Oceans was safely away, Osei sat down and crossed his legs at the ankles and tried to relax while he awaited his fate. He had no regrets. He had made his peace. In his own way, he had said goodbye to his family. He reminisced about some of the things he had done over the years like the presentation he had made at the Baptist church with the pastor's blessings. He had worried about the congregation's reaction in the days before the impending speech. He hoped it would be positive, and he prepared his words carefully.

"The Jim Crow laws that we are faced with are just another form of slavery that limits our freedom as African descendants," he counseled. "We must, we can, and we should push back against them. They tell us where we can eat, sleep, drink, walk, even use the toilet. They give us inferior schools, books, jobs, and living areas. They control our lives! Even though we're off the plantation, we still have a master. Soon they'll be trying to tell us who to marry. We must be resistant, rebellious, and defiant if we are to get our just rights. Push back, brothers and sisters. Push back. Challenge these unjust laws that only apply to colored people and not to so-called whites."

The acceptance of the speech was minimal—a few amens here and there—and ever since then, people had been looking at him as a troublemaker. It had caused him a lot of stress and anxiety, but he had tried not to show it. Sixteen-year-old Oceans seemed to be his only convert.

Now sitting in his cell knowing that he was soon to be lynched, he thought about all the wisdom that had been passed down through the years from generation to generation and ancestor to ancestor. All of which he knew he would not live to pass down to his children.

He descended from one of the most revered fighters in West Africa and leader of the last army to be defeated by the British. The British had tried and failed to destroy their history by burning and stealing, but it lived on through Obiri and others like him. It was kept alive by raising their family with the knowledge of their history—knowledge that he tried to pass along to his neighbors, but they refused to listen. He saw himself as an emissary of Africa, reaching out to African descendants from all parts of Africa who had forgotten or rejected their ancestry, carrying the word to remember their heritage, and reminding each one that it belonged to them by reason of birth. Because of this, he was seen as out of touch with the times. Now if at all possible, he would go down fighting just like one of those Ashante warriors who were so vicious. He refused to be docile even before the KKK death squad.

Late that same evening, one of the guards came into the cell room and yelled for him to come over to the bars. He continued to sit on the edge of his cot, looking meek and defeated but feeling full of fire and viciousness. A sensation of déjà vu came over him, and he had the illusion that he had lived this before. The guard called again, demanding that he obey. His resistance was steadfast. He just sat there as if he didn't hear him. Next, he heard the key in the cell door lock and knew what the guard had in mind. "No nigger ignores or disobeys me and gets away with it," the guard growled angrily, approaching his cot with his nightstick raised.

Obiri waited until he was near the cot, and then his right leg shot out, catching the guard right at the kneecap. There was a loud snap and a scream as the joint broke. The guard dropped his nightstick as he lost his balance and fell to the floor. Obiri the imaginary Ashante warrior was on him instantly, grabbed the billy club and started beating him across the head, neck, and shoulders with all his strength, showing no mercy.

The other guard, hearing the commotion, rushed into the cell, but Obiri was blind with the bloodlust and rage passed down by his ancestors, and before the guard could do anything, he cracked him across the knees with the club and beat him down to the floor—so full of fury that he continued to beat them both mercilessly until they stopped moving. He knew they were dead, but he felt no remorse—they were going to kill him anyway.

Finally, his rage starting to subside and thinking clearly, he decided what to do. He dragged the bodies out of his cell and put the billy club back into the first guard's hand. Then using the bottom of the thin mattress on his cot, he cleaned up the bloody mess in his cell and put the mattress back on his cot. He thought about escaping but knew that if he did, after killing two white men, they would kill his whole family, and he didn't have time to get them away before the men were discovered. The KKK may also get in a killing rage and murder other innocent colored families. He couldn't take a chance on that happening. He decided to try to create a mystery as to how the guards died. He took the guard's cell keys, reentered his cell, and locked it then tossed the keys back out of his cell where the guards lay.

He was sleeping peacefully when the sheriff arrived and discovered the bodies.

"Goddamn! Sheriff, come over here quick! Call an ambulance!"

"What's all the excitement?" the sheriff snapped stepping over near the cell then, "Ahhh shit, what happened here?"

"It looks like they've been beaten."

"Is the prisoner still here?"

"He's in his cell sleeping."

"Sleeping! Get that nigger up and find out what happened here."

When they questioned him, he answered, "I don't know. I stay out of white folks' business. It ain't nothing but trouble."

"You know something, and you better tell us. Did some of your friends do this?"

"If they did, I wouldn't still be here, would I?"

Don't get smart with me, damn it."

"What are you gonna do, lynch me?"

"You already got that coming."

"Well, no matter what I say, you can only lynch me once, so get out of my face. I've got nothing to say to you. If you want to find out what happened, figure it out for yourself."

"We'll beat it out of you if we have to," the sheriff threatened.

"You can beat me, but I ain't got nothing to say."

The mysterious and baffling murder of two deputies spread through Caloosa. The superstitious believed that Obiri somehow orchestrated the killings even though as far as they knew, he never left his cell. Even the sheriff was leery of him and believed that the sooner he was lynched, the better off they would be.

Suddenly none of his deputies wanted to guard him at night. Now Wesley Simmons, the KKK grand dragon whom he had beaten, was saying lynch him immediately.

The second night after the killings, a mob of KKK members took Obiri out of jail and lynched him. According to rumors started by one of the anonymous KKK members, Obiri was torched and castrated before being set on fire, and he never flinched, cried out, or begged for his life. The lynchers, except for the grand dragon, got little satisfaction out of killing a man who didn't seem to care. His body was left hanging from a tree on display for all to see.

Ocean's father, Enoch, and several other colored men who had the stomach for it sneaked into the woods after midnight and removed the body and gave him a martyr's burial in the black cemetery. His cause of death, instead of lynching—according to their religion—it was crucifixion.

Although Oceans was only sixteen years old, he begged to go, and his father—against his mother's wishes—finally gave in and let him go. Osei Obiri had been his friend and taught him many things about his beliefs, his village, and the Ashante Empire. Obiri's lynching hit Oceans hard. His admiration for the heroic way Osei had died was only equaled by his hatred for the grand dragon and the KKK that he represented. Someday and he didn't know how when, he would revenge the evil and injustice that the KKK stood for.

As Oceans mourned the terrible death of his friend and mentor, his father mourned the horrible events that caused such a dramatic change in his son's life.

Oceans started to change after Osei Obiri's lynching. He became more aggressive and prone to engage in unprovoked hostility. If somebody looked at him funny, he wanted to know what the problem was and was ready to fight. He was defiant, outspoken against white domination in general. If it was something he didn't like, he verbalized it loud and clear, the KKK in particular. He became unpredictable, quicker to fight, especially white boys his age. He became more competitive, forceful, assertive, and militant. He went to KKK headquarters and broke out all of the windows, made sneak attacks against covert KKK members.

His father, Enoch, saw the change and tried to talk to him. "Son, sit down over there on the couch for a minute. I know you feel rage, hate, and you want revenge. We all do, but you're not thinking straight. Things will change, but I want you to live to see it. It won't help you to get yourself lynched because Osei Obiri was lynched. Use your head, boy. If you just have to do something, make plans first. Don't go off half-cocked. Do it secretly, but not yet. Keep them guessing, but not yet. It's more disturbing and fearful to them if they don't know who's doing it. They won't know who to blame or where to look. It'll provoke fear and distrust, but it's not time yet. You're too young."

"But, Dad, if not now, when?"

"When the time is right—you'll know."

Oceans listened and took his father's council to heart and decided to bide his time. In tribute to Obiri, Oceans tried to mentor his son, Yeboa, and his daughter, Owusu Ansa, who was being teased at school because of their African names. He became their protector and big brother. Their mother, Asantehemaa Afua, soon became friends with Oceans's mother and father—Hester and Enoch.

CHAPTER 2

Now, nine years later, Oceans was coming home to Caloosa, Mississippi, after fighting in World War 2 at age twenty-four. He had a mantra, and he had been repeating it as he drove down the highway. The time was right!

It was the year 1945. The war was finally over, and Oceans was ending the most bizarre war history for a black man in World War 2. He had spent the entire war fighting with a French guerilla outfit resisting the German invasion of France. This was not the typical war history for a colored man in World War 2. It happened entirely by accident.

The American army was segregated, and most of the leaders were prejudiced against colored soldiers. They didn't even want them in the army and even manufactured lies then embellished them to Keep Negroes out. To make matters worse, white solders didn't respect them and even added to the deception by refusing to fight beside them. An Army War College study—made by biased officers repeating lies about the intelligence, courage, willingness, and ability of black men to fight—had deemed the Negro as inferior, lacking courage, unable to face danger, cowardly, and untrustworthy in battle in spite of the many times the Negro solders had proven themselves in previous wars. The label still stuck. Throughout the Seven Years' War (1756–1763), War of 1812 (June 1812–February 1815), Civil War (April 1861–May

1865), Indian Wars (1860–1890), World War 1 (July 1914–1918), a commendable history of the truth were told, such as the exploits of the Tenth Cavalry "Buffalo Soldiers," but fiction interfered with the facts, and fiction was the victor.

In boot camp, all colored soldiers were segregated and put into separate barracks away from the white recruits. They felt alienated and frustrated and became short tempered, argumentative, and combative. Unfortunately, they took their frustration out on each other. The equal treatment that they had foolishly expected when they joined the army was nonexistent. They faced the same Jim Crow laws that plagued them as civilians. As a result, the least little thing ended in trouble. They fought the white recruits whenever the opportunity presented itself. They needed something to focus their hostility on, so they chose Oceans's name. Funny how trivial matters can become important. One of the soldiers said his name was stupid and another said, "Not if he lived near the ocean."

"You're all wrong," he corrected, trying to keep it light. "I was the only Ocean in or near Caloosa."

"Well, there must have been a reason. I mean, nobody just names their child Oceans."

"There was a reason. My mother always wanted to see the Atlantic and the Pacific and couldn't, so she named me Oceans."

That explanation defused the situation, and everybody was satisfied. But the truce didn't last long. Finally, Oceans decided to put a stop to it for good. "Look. I'm tired of this shit. We're all black, and we're fighting each other. My name is Oceans. Get over it. Save your fighting for the Germans. That's who we're training to fight. If you want to get upset about something, get upset about spending hours on KP duty peeling potatoes and stinking onions while the white boys are training or relaxing, waiting impatiently for us to get chow ready so they can eat.

"Get mad about standing watches over empty dumpsters or empty barracks while the white boys sleep. If that don't make you mad, then nothing should. Now, the next one of you black sumbitches that starts some shit about my name, I'm going to end it with a knuckle sandwich, and if you think I'm jiving, let's step outside, and we'll see."

"You know what, Oceans? You're almost right," proclaimed a recruit called Freddy. "If this shit wasn't so serious, I'd be laughing instead of teasing."

"What do you mean almost right?"

"I mean, I ain't black sumbitch. I'm brown."

"Aww, man, git out of here with that stuff," a few of them said in unison. They all laughed, and that ended the hostility.

Colored soldiers didn't get the intense training that their white counterparts got. They were too busy carrying out menial duties. It was like it didn't matter if they were killed. Their main weapons were mops, potato peelers, kitchen knives, dishwater, and picks and shovels for digging latrines and any other menial jobs that could be found. Even with that, some of them did well in combat training and marksmanship. Some adapted to the training so well that they far out maneuvered their white counterparts. Their tactical exercises were skillful and confident to the dismay of white recruits. The drill sergeants were encouraging them to be more like the Negroes. They owned the parade grounds and the war games. This led to even greater alienation between the races.

Oceans had a natural ability with firearms and was the best among the blacks. Even though it wasn't acknowledged, he outshot most of the white recruits too and was among the few, white or colored, who qualified as an expert in marksmanship; he scored high on all of the Army General Classification test also, which surprised them. Still when he and the other colored boys were deployed after boot camp they went to mess duty, motor pools, or other menial duties. Unknown to him and the rest of the black recruits, the army had deliberately gauged the test to higher educational levels to weed out most black recruits whose educational level was fourth grade compared to eighth grade for whites.

Although Oceans hadn't gone to college, his father was an educated man for all the good it did him in Mississippi. He had completed high school and a year of college and believed the key to real freedom was learning. He had taught Oceans how to read and write before he was five years old. He taught him math, English, science, and history. "You can never know too much," he preached. Even though he had to work in the white school at night as a janitor, he didn't let that hold him back.

He spent hours in the school library after school was out, increasing his knowledge until the day when he could use it. He sneaked books home that were not available in the black school so that Oceans could have access to more information and a better education.

"I don't know if it will be in my lifetime, but we've got to be ready," he always said. "We got to be ready. Someday this knowledge will be worth something to you and to me if it's God's will."

"Not if the KKK has anything to say about it," Oceans would answer.

"I didn't say if it's the Klan's will. Have faith. It won't always be like this, son. They can deny you the proper education, but if you get it, they can't take it back. They can't lynch it out of you. They can't beat it out. They can't cut it out. It's yours for life."

His father was wise enough to know that education shouldn't be all work and no play, so one weekend while Oceans was in high school, he brought home a book on mimicry and ventriloquism. Oceans was so intrigued by it that he couldn't put it down. He realized that he had a unique talent for remembering voices and being able to mimic any voice or sound after hearing it only once. He studied and practiced the techniques of ventriloquism until he not only could speak and make his voice sound as though it was coming from somewhere else but he also barely moved his lips while doing it. He kept his friends and family in stiches as he entertained them with his ability to mimic different voices. He would go to his room and practice mimicking different white voices every chance he got.

"Practice, practice, practice," his father said one day. "Even though you can sound white, you can't be white, so what's all the practice for?"

"I don't know, Dad. I just feel like someday it will come in handy."

Oceans was well prepared for the test the army gave recruits, and If he had been a white boy, he would have qualified for officer training. Since he was black, they made him a truck driver. There was a rumor that another Negro by the name of Robinson was going to Officer Training School, but they didn't believe it. Oceans was assigned the job of driving supplies to the white troops on the front line. On the other hand, the white recruits who qualified as experts were sent to sniper school, and those with high test grades were sent to OTS even though their other test scores were much lower than his. The base commandant told Oceans that colored boys weren't smart enough for sniper school, and he probably just got some lucky shots on the gun range anyway, and when Oceans mentioned being an officer, he just laughed and didn't even answer.

Just the fact that Oceans had the nerve to question his assignment made the commanding officer mad. In many ways, colored soldiers, were treated worse than the enemy. After all, the Germans were white, which they were reminded of often either by words or deeds. There were white-only restaurants that German prisoners of war could eat in and black soldiers were forbidden to enter. Still, the black soldiers carried out their duties as assigned.

After arriving at the war zone, Oceans joined the other colored men in the motor pool, driving supplies to the front line. Even though he was disappointed, Oceans approached his assignment without complaint. He tried to get his supplies to the soldiers on the front line in a timely manner. Once he even drove through a bombardment with shells flying all around his truck and arrived with the supplies just as they were running out. The officer in charge was surprised that he made it and praised his commitment. He even commented to his fellow white officers that he was surprised that a black man would be that devoted to duty considering the way they were treated. The shelling was so bad that the other trucks turned back, but Oceans was determined to get through.

He soon had a reputation for getting the supplies through no matter what. When there was an emergency delivery, the commanders asked for Oceans because they knew he would get through. On one occasion, while trying to drive ammunition to the front line, his truck ran over a land mine and blew up. One minute he was driving and dodging potholes and explosions all around him, and the next his truck was flying through the air and coming apart. He heard a giant explosion, then suddenly everything was quiet.

Miraculously he lived through the explosion. He didn't know how long he had been unconscious, but when he woke up, he found himself listening to soldiers speaking German. As groggy as he still was, he recognized the fact that he was in German hands. They had other prisoners, and all of them were thrown into a truck.

He was like a zombie during the long ride to the POW camp ran by a Vichy regime somewhere in northern France. He didn't remember much about it except he thought it would never end.

Oceans was the only colored man among mostly white prisoners, southern rednecks, and a few captured Frenchmen from the French underground. To the Frenchmen, the Germans and most of the whites except the rednecks, he was just another prisoner. To the white southerners, he was a nigger boy and shouldn't live in the same space with the white prisoners. They didn't want to associate with him, nor did they want to eat at the same table or sleep in the same room, but of course, there was nothing they could do about that. He heard the word *nigger* a few times but didn't expect anything less, so he didn't respond. Past experience had taught him that bigotry and narrow-mindedness was inbred in these young racists. He had to constantly choke down his rage and resentment and remind himself that this wasn't the time. Even in a German prison, poor white trash thought he was inferior to them. That was a laugh. In this German prison, like it or not, they were equal. He tried to make the best of it. The prison was bad enough without adding to it.

But things finally reached the breaking point, and he couldn't take the malicious, sneering racist remarks any longer. The one they called Jetro was doing most of the talking while the others backed him up. He was big, and he thought he was bad. He had mistaken Oceans's passiveness for fear, and one day, he made the mistake of pushing him. Oceans surprised him with a vicious roundhouse right to the jaw that rocked him back on his heels followed by a savage elbow that cracked his jaw and knocked him off his feet.

Surprise and pain clouded his face and shot through his jaw, making his head spin. Somehow he rose to his feet, the other southerners egging him on. He threw a weak right as he staggered trying to keep his balance. It was more to buy some time to recover than to injure. Oceans moved in and threw a right jab that landed squarely on Jetro's nose, turning the puffed and bloodied face into pulp. Blood shot all over him. Jetro grunted and hit the floor on his back. Oceans stepped in fast and straddle him, smashing five quick blows to his cheek and eyes, blackening both of them. Somebody pulled him off Jetro and held his arms while Jetro staggered up and somehow found the strength to throw two stiff blows into Oceans's kidneys. Oceans broke loose and showered a flurry of lefts and rights into Jetro's midsection as he stumbled back, trying to stay on his feet and block the gut-busting punches. As Jetro started to fall, he showed no mercy, hammering him with two rights and a left hook, tearing part of his right ear and leaving it hanging.

Dazed, Jetro went down breathing hard but still game enough to throw a wild punch into naked air. Oceans finished it by nailing him with a wicked roundhouse to the head, slamming the back of Jetro's head against the floor and putting him out for good.

"Okay. Who's next?" he asked, stumbling back and facing the other rednecks whose faces seemed to have gotten a deeper red. "I tried to keep my peace, but you wouldn't let me." He decided to throw a little shit in the game. They might just buy it. "Remember, anything you can do to me, I can do to you too. Oh yeah, if anyone decides to visit my bunk one night while I'm sleep, leave a suicide note on your bunk. I'll have a surprise for you. Don't forget—all closed eyes ain't sleep, and all sleep ain't sound. I listen with a third ear and see with a third eye. And, Jetro, if you're back with us, just remember there's more where that came from.

"Don't believe all that stupid propaganda the generals put out about black men. I'll fight faster than you, harder than you, and better than you. I'll hurt, maim, and kill. I'll show everything but mercy. There's no yellow on me, all black."

When it was over, it was clear to everyone that they had underestimated him. It felt good to prove to these bigots that his inferiority was only in their imaginations. Still, he didn't come out of the fight unscathed.

The French prisoners and German guards had just looked on and didn't interfere. To them, this was rare entertainment. There were no more problems with the young rednecks after the fight. German guards and the French prisoners continued to treat him as an equal even though they sometimes made it clear that they wanted to be alone.

It didn't take Oceans long to realize that this prison was a gold mine of languages for a person who had the ability to remember and speak languages and dialects like a native. He could repeat everything he heard, but he didn't always know what they were saying, so he would ask a German guard or a French prisoner what does this mean or what does that mean. As a teen, he had discovered that he had the ability to mimic sounds and speech after hearing them only once.

"It's a God-given gift," his father had once told him. As a child, he had mimicked friends, teachers, and movie stars. "You can learn anywhere and from anyone."

Oceans listened intently to the German and French speech patterns, dialects, accents, and even vernacular and slang. For him, it was like a schoolroom where learning never stopped, and he took advantage of it. When he was alone, he practiced quietly and slowly became proficient. It didn't take him long to be able to sound like them and use some of their mannerisms. Over the few months that he was imprisoned, he even picked up some of the white southern nuances that the white prisoners used when talking among themselves. He was surprised at how quickly he picked up the languages, and it was a good thing because they spoke freely in front of him since they were unaware that he now understood much of what they were saying. He even used his ventriloquism to poke fun at the rednecks.

One day, he said to the worst of the lot, "I think that colored guy is a lot smarter than you are" and made it sound like one of his friends said it. Oceans was the only one who knew what the fight was about. One of the fighters didn't even know.

He soon found out why the Frenchmen would shut him out sometimes. They were planning an escape. He didn't let on that he knew but watched them and found out they had been digging a tunnel for the last six months, and it was almost ready. The American whites didn't seem to know about it, and he wasn't gonna tell them. He knew the escape was imminent, but he didn't know when.

But even more importantly and surprisingly, he heard one of the Frenchmen speaking to a German guard in German and that he was actually a German plant put there to report on the activities of the Frenchmen. He wondered if there was a spy with the whites also. The Germans knew all about the French escape and would be waiting at the end of the tunnel when the Frenchmen came out. He knew the Frenchmen wouldn't believe him if he told them, and he might end up being killed in his sleep, so he waited.

On the night of the escape, he followed them through the tunnel. For the first time in his life, he had doubts about his ability. In the short time he had been in the army, he had never killed anyone. He wanted to rescue the Frenchmen, but in order to do that, he had to attack the German soldiers. All he had was a heavy stick that he found in the tunnel and was using as a club. He had never had to face being killed before and hoped he wouldn't panic or freeze. He didn't think he would, but this was the first time he would be facing a trained soldier in close combat, and he was a little afraid, but he had to do this. He couldn't let them be recaptured. All this went through his mind in seconds. He hastily planned his strategy. He would quickly and quietly attack the last guard and get his gun then start shooting the other guards. He was depending on the prisoners to realize what was going on and attack the other guards. It all sounded so simple.

Then he was at the end of the tunnel and heard the German guards as they overpowered the unsuspecting prisoners when they came out of the tunnel and started marching them back to the POW camp. He disregarded his apprehension and slipped out of the exit, forgetting his fear and moving quietly and attacking the last guard viciously. Grabbing his rifle, he started shooting the other guards. Realizing what was happening, the prisoners reacted, swiftly disarming and shooting the remaining guards. In seconds, it was over and they started to run. After a while, they heard the dogs behind them, but the Frenchmen had planned for the dogs, and those that they couldn't evade, they killed. The German soldiers chasing them never even came close.

Once they got away from the area and reached French resistance headquarters, they turned to Oceans.

"How did you know about our escape plans?"

Oceans answered them in their own language. "I just listened to you as you made them," he smiled.

The surprise on their faces was priceless. "We were so careful to speak only among ourselves," their leader, Quentin, contended.

"Yet it's good that you did find out," he said, speaking in English, "and even luckier that you came out behind us instead of with us."

"It wasn't luck. I knew the Germans would be waiting."

"But how could the Germans have found out?"

"You were betrayed. One of your men is a German spy."

"A German spy? With us? Impossible!"

Finally their leader chuckled. "Too bad you didn't hear who betrayed us."

"I did," Oceans said calmly, turning his eyes toward the one called Philipp who started to back up. And speaking to him in German then saying in French, "It was this German agent planted with your group."

"C'est un mensonge!" he yelled. "That's a lie."

The other Frenchmen just turned toward Philipp, not saying anything. He became unnerved by the hostile stares and broke to run, a clear admission of his guilt. One of the Frenchmen that he had deceived calmly shot him.

"We owe you more than we can ever pay."

"You owe me nothing," Oceans assured them.

"At least we can help you get back to the American lines, but it might take a while."

"I would rather stay with you and see some action if I can, but I have to tell you that I've never been in combat."

"Since you rescued us, we know you will fight, but there will be no time to train you."

"I don't need training. I had combat training in boot camp. Just tell me what you want me to do, and I'll do it."

A squad of their comrades who were just returning from ambushing a German patrol was surprised to see that they had escaped.

"It's good to have you and your men back safe, Quentin," Nicolas, the underground leader, said to them as he laboriously walked back into camp. "But how did you do it. According to our intelligence, that prison is the most secure in Vichy France. Marshal Philippe Petain swears by it."

"If it wasn't for Oceans here, we wouldn't have made it. We were recaptured as soon as we got out, but Oceans followed us and attacked the Germans from behind. Now he wants to remain with us, but he's never been in combat."

"Didn't you say he rescued you?" Nicolas contradicted innocently.

"Yes. Why?"

"Then he's been in combat.

"He's your responsibility," Nicolas said to Quentin. "Make the best of it."

"Stay with me," Quentin cautioned Oceans. "You'll be okay. If we go one on one with the Germans, it's each man for himself, kill or be killed."

"Don't worry about me. I'm not ready to die."

They were out before dawn the next morning. A strategic village was under attack, and they couldn't allow it to be taken. Although they were a small force, the strategy was a sweeping surprise attack, killing as many Germans as possible and forcing them to retreat. Oceans decided to treat it like they were all Ku Klux Klansmen there to terrorize and lynch, and he attacked with the savage fierceness and brutality of a black man defen`ding his very existence. He was shooting and fighting man to man with complete disregard for his own safety, tearing though the German resistancelike a bloodthirsty fiend.

Suddenly the Germans started to retreat, but Oceans didn't let up, showed no mercy. In effect, he became a killing machine. When it was over and they regrouped, the Frenchmen had accepted him as one of them, in their actions but made no verbal comment, just looked at him with respect.

After his first battle, he continued to fight with purpose, courage, determination, and the attitude that all of the Germans were Klan.

Over the years that followed, Oceans had plenty of chances to use his language prowess.

The American army had him listed as missing in action even though they thought he was dead. They didn't know he had been taken prisoner and eventually escaped from prison or that he was still alive, but they found out later that there was a colored American fighting with the French underground.

Fighting behind the lines, Oceans learned many of the Germans invasion and attack plans and passed them on to the Americans as soon as possible, saving many American lives. He used the code name *Oceans T,* hoping they would recognize that it was Oceans Tires.

Living and fighting with Frenchmen, he heard nothing but French and became very fluent in the language. Over the next few months and years, he learned to fight with every weapon, including knives and clubs and bare hands, but acting as a sniper with his rifle was his most effective weapon.

Sometimes he would think about his life as a prisoner of Jim Crow and the KKK. It was even more devastating than the German POW camp even though there was no physical fences. There were overwhelming mental barriers caused by the Jim Crow laws and the fear of KKK and their terrifying night raids and reprisals. What was so mind-boggling was the physical distance this prison covered. Getting free of it wasn't as simple as digging a tunnel a few hundred yards because it covered a whole section of the southern United States encompassing many states. This was what he had to look forward to at the end of the war. Racism and discrimination was his reward. He would leave the minefields here to go home and try to avoid the racial minefields there. His thoughts were interrupted by a sudden attack.

The sounds were deafening. Suddenly they were under attack. The German fire was heavy. Bullets were bouncing and ricocheting all around them. They had been surprised. Two men went down. Only one got up. The other one was dead. Soldiers were cussing, yelling, crying, killing, and dying, but at least they could fight back. Shells were exploding, and shrapnel was flying.

Oceans jumped up and ran zig-zag to a shack that was half blown apart. Then a grenade was thrown. It landed so close to him that he could see the markings on it. He quickly snatched it up and threw it back. It exploded right in a German machine gun nest. Just as quickly, it was quiet again. The attack was over as suddenly as it started, and they cautiously moved on. A few hundred yards farther on, a sniper started firing. Two more men went down. There were only three of them left. It was a bad spot. The sniper shot again, and another man went down. To move would have been suicidal, but if they didn't move, he was going to kill them all. They didn't know which way to go because he hadn't been spotted and to stick your head up to look was sure death. Something had to be done, but what? No one wanted to be a hero or a martyr trying to save the others and themselves.

They were in a tight fix. The first thing that came to Oceans's mind was to use his unique ability to mimic sounds and voices. During his childhood, he had spent many hours entertaining his friends with this unique gift. Now it occurred to him that imitating a German just might save their lives.

Over the last few months, he had become pretty proficient in speaking the language and could sound exactly like one of them. "Don't shoot! We are friends!" he abruptly called out in German, startling and surprising his companions. "We are friends!" he continued to yell in German.

The shooting stopped, and there was sudden movement in one of the trees ahead. Oceans aimed and shot. All at once, a German sniper stood and tumbled off his perch. He had been well camouflaged with branches and leaves, and they never would have seen him. The gimmick had worked, and just like that, the shooting was over. They were lucky to be alive. This colored man who's courage they had heard American white men question and say so many disparaging things about had once again saved their lives.

Oceans stood, went over, and looked down at the dead sniper but felt no sympathy. After all, he was the enemy—he was Klan. One he wouldn't have to worry about. The German was still clutching his rifle. Oceans reached down and took the rifle out of his hands. It was an American-made Springfield 1903-A4 with an M73 scope. Now he finally had what America wouldn't give him—a real sniper rifle—and ironically, he got it from a German.

He briefly wondered where the German sniper had gotten an American sniper rifle but knew he would never know. Maybe this was just one more advantage that the Germans had over colored GIs. He wiped the dust and leaves off and threw it over his shoulder. Finally, he was a sniper.

It didn't take long for him to put his new rifle into action. Oceans focused his eyes on the unsuspecting German colonel in the distance. Then he leaned down and sighted through the M73 scope on the 1903-A4 Springfield rifle. It was like standing across the street from him. He slowly put pressure on the trigger and, seconds later, watched the colonel slowly crumble to the ground, never knowing what hit him. His men dived for cover, but their leader was the only target. The colonel's loss would throw his crack unit into chaos.

Over the next few years, he put his sniper skills to good use.

They had just come back from a raid, and they were all tired and worn out. They had lost two men, and even though loses were common, their spirits were low. Word was that a platoon of American soldiers had been ambushed and was surrounded and trapped by Germans. Oceans volunteered to take a group out and try to rescue them.

Not knowing that help was on the way, the captain leading the platoon looked over his situation hopelessly. The bombardment had ceased, but the Germans were all around them shooting at anything that moved. As far as he could see, there was no way out, especially with all of his dead and wounded. Then the shooting stopped, and he figured the Germans were preparing to ask him to surrender—either that or getting ready for the final rush. He didn't want to surrender, but it seemed inevitable if he wanted to save the rest of his men.

He decided to wait a few more minutes before making a decision and then reevaluate. Then he heard a single shot from a long way off followed by several others.

When Oceans and his men got there, he saw that the Americans were totally locked in. While his men took their positions, Oceans started a deadly sniper attack, killing several German officers and men.

The Germans were scattering and looking behind them. For the next few minutes, the captain heard shot after shot. A sniper was picking the Germans off one by one.

Then the rest of Oceans's group opened up from strategic positions. It sounded like a whole division was attacking the German position. The Germans were under attack by somebody. The captain couldn't imagine who. He knew there were no other American units in this sector.

The Germans soon started to retreat. Between his men and the mystery attacking force, the Germans were taking heavy fire.

When he was sure the Germans had moved out of range, Oceans left his perch and slowly approached the American position.

The captain had started to reorganize his men when they looked up and saw an optical illusion. Coming over the hill was a Negro soldier swinging a sniper rifle. As he came, he yelled out orders to his men in French. "Set up a perimeter and send out scouts to make sure they're gone! See if you can commandeer a German truck for these men. I think they're going to need it.

"I hope your loses weren't too great, captain," Oceans said walking up. "We got here as fast as we could."

"That uniform. You're an American soldier?"

"Yes sir."

"Who are you? Where did you come from? What are you doing out here? What's your outfit?"

"Slow down, captain. It's a long story, and that's a lot of questions. Where do you want me to start?

"I've been fighting with the French underground since I was captured by the Germans and escaped in 1941. I was in the motor pool before my truck was blown up, and I was captured. When I escaped with a few French soldiers, I just stayed with them."

"What's your name, soldier?"

"Oceans Tires from Mississippi, sir."

"Here I am asking you a lot of questions when I should be saying thanks for saving our bacon. I was just so surprised to see a Negro out here fighting with the French."

"If I was with my unit, I'd be driving a truck or digging latrines in spite of being a sharpshooter and scoring high on the army evaluation exams."

"You scored high on the exams and the gun range?"

"Yes, sir, I did."

"What did the commanding officer say about that?"

"He said it was an accident then assigned me to the motor pool."

"What do you think he should have done?"

"I should have gone to Officers Candidate School, and if I was white, I would have. But the least I should have gotten was sniper school."

"Where did you get that sniper rifle?"

"Took it off a German sniper."

"A German? Where did he get it?"

"I couldn't even guess, sir."

"Well, I think you would have made a good officer. I'll make sure the American forces know who you are and what you're doing out here. You deserve a medal for what you've done. In the meantime, sergeant, I'm giving you a battlefield promotion, and I'll make sure the brass knows you earned it."

"Thank you, sir."

"No! Thank you, sergeant."

Oceans heard a white soldier say in the background, "Can you believe this? I never thought I'd be saved by a nigger and a uppity nigger at that, and now he's a sergeant. I thought the word was that they were scared to fight and couldn't be trusted."

"Looks like the word was wrong," another soldier said.

"Well, I just don't like owing my life to a nigger."

"Maybe you'd rather be dead or captured."

"When you put it like that, I don't care who he is. I'm just glad he got us out of this mess."

"To tell you the truth, I didn't know we had any Negro snipers in this man's army," one of the white soldiers said to Oceans.

"Well, I'm not official. I took this rifle off a German sniper—how he got it I wouldn't know. I tried to get one when I came out of boot camp, but they told me my shooting was all luck, then the army put me on a truck hauling supplies. Said Negroes wasn't smart enough to be snipers."

"They need to rewrite that communication," the sergeant put in. "You speak French, but you sound like you from the south."

"Like I told the captain, I'm from Mississippi."

For the next couple of hours, Oceans was telling the captain how he got there. When he finished, the captain just looked at him for a minute. "Why did you stay with the French underground?"

"The American army don't allow Negroes on the front line. The French do."

"Would you like to come back to our lines?"

"The Americans don't allow Negroes on the front line."

"I guess the army underestimated a lot of you negro GIs. I can understand it. I've seen the War College studies. I think you're doing a fine job out here, sergeant. Keep up the good work."

"Thank you, sir!"

"Now, can you help us get back to our lines?" the Captain asked.

When the captain told Oceans his name, it was the same as one of the generals', and he wondered if they could be related.

Over the next several months, Oceans and his group had numerous other skirmishes as the war started to wind down. He continued to use the sniper rifle and the mimicry and became more proficient with both. By the time the war was over, he was accurate up to over 700 yards. The sniper rifle became like a third arm to him. He soon became one of the leaders planning and carrying out raids against the Germans. By the end of the war, he learned a lot about fighting and surviving. He had faced danger and death many times.

He even sent back a few intelligence reports about coming attacks on American units and signed his name to them. When the fighting was over and he got back to the American lines, he hoped they would recognize his name from the information he had sent back—some saving many American lives. He expected to have trouble drawing his back pay, but he didn't. The paymaster paid him all of his back pay with a frown, but no questions and, to his surprise, paid his sergeant's pay also. Now he was sure that the captain who promoted him was the son of one of the generals'. They could have tried him for desertion since he never tried to get back to the Allied lines, but that didn't happen either. He figured the captain he rescued had something to do with that too. It's good to have a general in your corner especially if you're black.

Now he was returning home to Mississippi to fight a new war and old enemies, Jim Crow and the KKK. But he was ready for the hate and hostility that this adversary would bring.

While fighting with the French, he realized for the first time that he was blessed with the intelligence to accomplish anything he set his mind to. Living under the caste system had given him many doubts about himself, his manhood, and abilities. It took the French and the war to wake him up. At home, even though he called himself a man, white domination made him feel like a boy.

WELCOME TO ENGLAND, NIGGERS

After the miracle of getting his five years' back pay from the U.S. Army for being missing in action, Oceans finally arrived in England, his last stop before heading home to the States. He expected and had planned for the war against Jim Crow and the KKK but was unprepared for the vicious physical and verbal attacks being perpetrated against black GIs in England by racist white GIs.

After fighting for freedom and equality for countries thousands of miles from home, black GIs now realized that fighting for their country hadn't changed a thing, hadn't even earned them the same rights at home. They were still second-class citizens.

It would be a few days before the troop ship left for the United States, so he checked in with the host family that he had been billeted with and headed for the nearest pub for some refreshments. A disturbance caught his attention up the street, and when he got near the pub, he realized that several white GIs were attacking a lone black GI and calling him names. Grabbing a brick, which was the nearest weapon he could find, he charged into the fray determined to help the lone black GI, not even fully understanding why this was happening because he hadn't been in England long enough to understand how deeply that racism was entrenched or, for that matter, that it even existed between American GIs in England.

He heard some yelling and looked back to see another group of white men running toward them. They couldn't get away, so Oceans braced for the beating that was inevitable. However, to his surprise, the new group attacked the white GIs and rescued them. Now, both sides were confused. Oceans was confused and the white GIs who attacked them were baffled.

"These black GIs helped to save our country just as you did, and we will not allow them to be mistreated or discriminated against. Come on over to the pub. Let us buy you a drink."

Oceans and his new friend went but reluctantly. The white GIs in the pub gave them intimidating looks, but there were no incidents. Once they had gotten away, Oceans made light of the situation by asking the soldier whose name he now knew was McDaniels, "What did you do, talk about somebody's mommy? You must have just shipped in."

"Got here today."

"I thought so. Look, man, talk about racism. This place is worse than Mississippi, and I don't mean the British—they're on our side. I'm talking about American GIs, and the officers in charge are behind them. They've got this place so segregated that black GIs can't go anywhere. That's what caused the fight. That club is supposed to be off limits to colored soldiers, but I just decided the hell with it and went anyway. Funny I thought things would be different for colored people after the war. Now I realize that we fought to give other countries the freedom that we don't even have ourselves. The Germans have more freedom in our country then we do.

"Can you believe England welcomed us back with open arms? America welcomed us back with balled fist. I feel like finding a lone white GI and beating the hell out of him, but what's the use? You can beat the hell out of a man, but you can't beat the hate out of him."

"Damn! Forget this shit. Come on, Oceans—man, that's a funny name—let's get a beer in a place where we're welcome."

Two days later, he shipped out for the port of New York.

Colored soldiers were quartered in the bow of the ship—the forward part—which was the bumpiest ride during rough seas. They weren't surprised nor did they complain. They were just happy to be going home. In fact, the only surprise for Oceans was a pleasant one—his recent acquaintance, McDaniels, was sailing home on the same ship. Most of their time was spent sitting up on the forecastle (fo'c'sle) by the anchor winch with the other colored GIs discussing the changes fighting in the war had made in the status of the Negro. They all agreed that the total gain for the Negro after fighting in the war was zero.

Eventually they got around to talking about home and future plans. Oceans described the conditions Negroes lived under in his hometown of Caloosa, Mississippi, detailing the effects of Jim Crow and the terror of the KKK.

"Why don't all the colored folks get together and fight this KKK?" someone asked.

"We can't because they wear white sheets and hoods when they attack and we don't know who all of them are. If we did that, the ones we don't know would retaliate at night and kill a lot of innocent families."

McDaniels faced discrimination in New York, but nothing like Oceans described. "So why are you going back? Why don't you stay in New York? It's not great, but it's better than Mississippi."

"My family is there. Also, I want to do something about it."

"What can you do?"

"I think that if I can put fear into the KKK, everything else will get better too."

"How you gonna do that? You just one man."

"I think I've found a way to put fear into them without them knowing that I'm black."

"That don't make no sense, man, and you know it unless you figured out a way to turn yourself white, and that's impossible."

"That's it, Mac. You said it."

"I said what?"

"Turn myself white! I'll turn myself white."

"Now I know you done lost your damn mind."

Suddenly Oceans started speaking, using the voice of a white movie star that they both knew. All of the colored soldiers nearby turned around to face them, looking for a white face in their midst.

"Damn, O, I'm looking right at you, and I don't believe it. You sound just like Humphrey Bogart."

"I can sound like anybody I want to sound like."

"Okay, let's hear you sound like the captain."

Oceans did a perfect imitation of the captain's voice, mannerisms and all, and everybody on the fo'c'sel started laughing. For the next hour, he was doing everybody from the commanding officer to the ship's captain.

"Shit, man, you need to go to Hollywood, not Mississippi," McDaniels teased.

"Do you think we need more than one Stepin Fetchit?"

"Okay, man, you can sound white, but you still black."

"The KKK wear white sheets and hoods, so we can't tell who they are. What if I put on a sheet and hood and sound white, as far as anyone can tell, I'll be white."

Mac didn't say anything for a few minutes. Then he said, "If anybody snatches the hood off, you're dead, white boy."

Except for some rough seas, which frequently sent them to the side rail where they heaved and dry-heaved throwing up what little food they had managed to get down during the previous meal, the trip home was uneventful. Oceans disembarked in New York with a new friend and a renewed passion for fighting the Klan.

His friend, who was from New York, invited him to spend a few days with him, which he happily accepted. After two weeks of hitting clubs in Harlem, like the Cotton Club, Apollo, and the Savoy, and even learning the latest dances like the lindy hop, the jitterbug, the boogie-woogie, and the two-step, he was ready to go home to Caloosa.

"Mc Daniels where can I buy some black dye and black ink?"

"We can get that right down the street. What you gonna dye, buddy?"

"I figure if the KKK can wear white sheets and hoods, I can wear black. You know, white man, white sheet, black man, black sheet."

"Hope they don't put that shit together." He laughed. "If they do, yo ass is dead."

"I'll worry about that later. Now where can I buy some white sheets? I got some dyeing to do. I want to have those sheets ready to go as soon as I get home. You think your mother could sew me a hood with two eyeholes?"

"Let's ask her and find out."

A few days before his departure, McDaniels took him to a car lot where the salesman tried to rip him off, but he did manage to get the cost down quite a bit below the original price. Even so, he still got the colored discount and not the white markdown.

He finally left New York with two black sheets and two hoods with eyeholes. He was ready to become his alter ego at a moment's notice.

While Oceans was having fun in New York and learning new dances, unknown to him his future antagonist Wesley Simmons, the grand dragon of the local KKK in his home town of Caloosa, was declaring his candidacy for mayor.

Before Oceans left, his friend advised him to get one of those Negro travel books to be on the safe side. "Anyway, a black man driving down these racist highway needs all of the help he can get, and my cousin says this book saved his life. I think it's called *The Green Book*. Anyway, it's supposed to tell you what gas stations, restaurants, and stores cater to colored on the highway. It even tells you which towns have curfews for Negros. You may need it before you get to Mississippi. He says that some colored drivers even buy a chauffeur's cap so that if they get stopped by the Klan, they can say they're going to pick up their white boss."

Oceans refused to stoop that low.

"Better to stoop low than to swing high if you get my meaning. If you won't get the book, at least put about four five-gallon cans of gas in your trunk and take some baloney sandwiches, and my mother will fry you up some chicken."

"Don't worry about me!" Oceans urged, his tone almost irritated. "I'll be okay."

"Well, all right, It's your life."

Just as he was driving away the next morning, McDaniels ran up to the car and threw a package into the back seat. "A little something to remember me by!" he yelled. "Open it at your first rest stop."

He hated to leave his friend, but he had to get home. And he had a long way to go.

Driving from New York through New Jersey and part of Pennsylvania was fast and uneventful, but he finally had to pull off the highway and rest near the Ohio border. He thought about the mystery package Mac had thrown into the car and tore it open.

"My friend McDaniels," he said to himself as he picked up *The Green Book* and tried the chauffeur's cap on for size. He rolled into Indiana with high hopes of

CHAPTER 3

Homecoming

The only Ocean in Mississippi was going home but much wiser, tougher, smarter, and more mature than he was when he left. He was still wearing his uniform but had the first civilian clothes he had purchased in five years on the seat next to him. New car, well, new to him anyway, new clothe and money in his pocket—more money than he ever had at one time thanks to his four years back pay from the army. He was proud of his uniform and wanted his mother and father to see him in it. In the trunk, he had his sniper rifle—a poignant reminder of his time in combat and of his future plans for the weapon. He was surprised at how much he still missed the fighting and his guerilla friends from the war. After fighting together and depending on each other for over four years, they had become very close. He never thought he'd be that close to a bunch of white guys. But then they were nothing like the white racist trash in Mississippi. Still, he had three good old friends at home that he was anxious to see. He hoped they were still in Caloosa.

    He rounded a bend and went up a hill, all the time keeping his eye out for deer running across the road.

THE NIGHTMARE ON THE SIDE OF THE ROAD

Night caught him driving down a long dark road in Indiana. Somehow he had missed his turn and gotten off the main road. He yawned and heard his stomach growl for the umpteenth time. He was dead tired and decided to pull over, eat a bologna sandwich, and rest a few minutes. The night was warm and stuffy, and the breeze coming in through the window was so refreshing that it eventually lulled him to sleep. He was just too tried.

After a couple of hours, something woke him up. When he sat up and looked out the windshield, he thought he saw a campfire in the woods and heard a scream, but who could be building a campfire way out there this time of morning? The scream came again. This time as if in terrible pain. *Somebody is in trouble,* he thought. *What if this is a lynching?* He couldn't just drive away. He had to know. Grabbing his rifle and after a slight hesitation, he grabbed his black sheet and hood. He got out and crept into the woods. It sounded like a lynching, but it couldn't be, not up north in Indiana.

His only fear was snakes. The insects and other night creatures were all quiet. Silently he sneaked into the woods and headed toward the fire. The only sound was a steady moaning from the camp. As he got closer to the fire, he could see shadows of men moving around in the firelight. It looked like someone was struggling, and he heard a voice begging, whimpering, and praying.

Moving very quietly, he walked between some tall trees and looked through a dense growth of shrubs. It was just as he suspected. Three trucks were parked in a clearing, surrounding a burnt-out tree. Several Klansmen were preparing to lynch a black man, but they hadn't tied him up yet. They were all around him taunting and poking with pointed, edged sticks and rifle barrels. One of them was intimidating him with a graphic description of what they intended to do to him. The look on his face was one of pure terror while the other faces that he could see showed pure pleasure. There was no way he would let this happen. He had to try and save him. The helpless victim let out another terrified scream that sent chills down his spine. His mission against the

Klan was unexpectedly starting early. Under no circumstances would he stand by and do nothing.

He heard one of them say, "This will teach you to stay in your place, nigger."

He quickly slipped the black sheet over his head and pulled the hood on. They had gotten so relaxed that some had taken off their sheets and hoods. This lynching was recreation for them, but not for their black victim. They even had jugs of whiskey.

"Quiet! I think I heard something," one of them slurred as he lowered the jug and walked directly toward Oceans.

When he squinted into the darkness, Oceans busted him in the face with the butt of his rifle then immediately changed his position. When their companion suddenly came flying back into the clearing with a busted face, it spooked them. Then a voice came out of the night and demanded that they drop their weapons and turn the colored man loose, alarming them even more.

Using the ventriloquism that he had perfected over the years, Oceans had thrown his voice so that it appeared to come from some place other than where he was standing. One of the men turned and fired several shots into the dark where the voice had come from. Angrily, he shouted back into the night, "Come out and let us see you, you coward! And we'll send you straight to hell, whoever you are!"

He was killed instantly by a shot out of the black. Oceans shot again when he saw one of them about to poke the prisoner with a red-hot rod, saving the colored man from more torture.

"Who's out there? Come in here where we can see you."

"Let that boy go!" Oceans demanded, stepping out into the clearing, his black hood and sheet barely visible!

"You sound like a white man! You should understand!" one of them shouted, still making no attempt to release the helpless victim. "This nigger raped my woman!"

"I didn't do it," the colored man blubbered.

"I say he did, and we're gonna kill him and you too, nigger lover," he said, turning his rifle and firing blindly toward the black apparition and missing.

Without another word, Oceans did what he should have done at first—started shooting instead of trying to reason with them. Two more of the men were hit and fell bleeding profusely. Two men ran into the woods. He could hear them crashing through the trees and vegetation, making funny groaning noises as they ran. When Oceans stepped farther into the clearing in his black sheet and hood, the remaining Klansmen cowered, throwing down their weapons in fear, too terrified to run.

In the blinking flames of the fire, he looked inhuman. "Next time there's a lynching, we're going to drag you and your family out of your home and lynch you all. Now get out of here before we start with you all tonight."

"You've suffered enough," he said, releasing the victim and reassuring him. "You're okay now. Can you walk?"

"I think so."

"Well, take one of these trucks and get the hell out of here," he advised.

"Who are you?"

"I'm a friend."

"Where did you come from?"

Ignoring the question, Oceans shouted to the free scared and confused Negro, "Get out of here, man, and out of the county too if you know what's good for you! And take your family with you."

"Okay, but who are you? You colored, but you sound white."

"Look, man, we don't have time to get acquainted. We gotta get out of here. No telling who heard those shots. You're free, you're alive, and it's up to you to stay that way. Now go. Get as far away from here as you can."

All of the time he was talking, Oceans was scooping up the Klan paraphernalia. "Ditch that truck as soon as you can," he suggested and started shooting up the other trucks up. The sheets they left would be put to good use—real authentic Klan garb. All he had to do now was wash and dye them black. A black sheet and hood and a white voice. Caloosa was in for a surprise it wouldn't like.

He got into his car and sped away, feeling justified and exhilarated. He had left three dead bodies behind him. Violence came too easy to him now. But there was no other way to save the colored man from torture and certain death by the KKK. His thoughts were like spoken words in his mind.

Still assured but cautious, he continuously checked the rearview mirror while looking for a way to get back to the main road. He knew it was much too soon for anybody to be after him even if they knew who he was. He also knew that he had to be alert because the Ku Klux Klan patrolled these roads looking for colored travelers to harass, and he didn't want to accidently run up on them, but if he did, he swore to himself that it would be their bad luck, not his. It didn't take him long to find his way back to the main highway.

For many years, he had thought about defying the KKK but didn't know how to do it without putting himself and his family in jeopardy. He knew that they would come after him if they knew who he was and, in the process, hurt other black people, but he had found a way to fight against them and do it without revealing his race. Of course, he couldn't stop the whole KKK, but maybe he could wipe out the chapter in his hometown of Caloosa. It was something to think about, he concluded. He now had a foolproof way to make it work.

There were no witnesses left back in that clearing. The one who got away had only heard him from behind the bushes using his white voice and didn't know he was colored. His identity was well protected. Confronting and frustrating the KKK, even this small group, had given him a great feeling of power and pride. He was elated but still apprehensive.

He checked the rearview again. Driving down the highway, he thought about the trouble he would be in if he was pulled over by the police, and they found him with the KKK paraphernalia. He would never be able to explain it. He decided right then that he would not go down easily. He would fight for his life.

Now that he knew that the KKK was active in Indiana, he stayed vigilant. A few cars passed him, but none were threating.

He was out of breath. His feet were raw. He was bleeding from several parts of his body, and on top of all that, he was naked and scared. Now he knew that he should have listened to that man and taken the truck. He was worn out but, thank God he was alive. As he approached his house, he saw that all of the lamps were lit. His wife, children, and several neighbors were standing outside. He covered himself as best he could. As he stumbled toward the house, they ran to meet him.

"Never expected to see you alive again," his wife cried. "It's a miracle!"

"How did you get away?" a neighbor asked.

"It's nothing but God!" his grandmother wailed.

When he fell, his brother picked him up and carried him the rest of the way. "Got to get out of here," he repeated over and over. "Got to get out before they come," he repeated incoherently.

Between breaths, he told them what happen as they listened in disbelief. "He killed three of them, but one got away."

His brother wanted to hear more. He had questions. "You mean he killed three white men? Who was he? Where did he come from? You say he was colored? Why would he take a chance on helping you? He could have been lynched too."

"Give him a chance to answer, Fred."

"Don't know. He just did. He was like a ghost. He came out of nowhere. I don't know why he stopped them."

His wife interrupted, "It was the grace of God, but where will we go? We got no money."

"We'll go to Jackson and stay with your aunt Ruth, then we go north. If we stay here, we're dead."

"He's right, Mary. You've got to run while you can. The Klan will never let this go. They'll be looking for revenge."

"Take my old truck," his brother offered. "I think it will make it. Leave it with Ruth, and I'll get up there and get it next week. Here, this is all of the money we got, but you're welcome to it, and there's gas in my truck. Maybe you can scrape up some more and take the train from Jackson."

Oceans had only gone a few miles when he saw the headlights in his rearview mirror coming up fast. At first, it scared him. He thought it was the police after him for what he did to the men trying to lynch the poor Negro man on the side of the road. He reached over and grabbed his rifle. *If they stop me, I'll stop them.*

But they swung around him at the last minute and started to pass. The white driver looked over at him as he passed and did a double take. *Fucking nigger,* he mouthed.

Now I know I'm back in the South, he thought to himself. *You don't know how lucky you are,* he mouthed to the back of the car, feeling like he could lick the world.

The rest of his trip through Indiana was uneventful, but he kept alert for trouble. He rejected the idea of stopping in Chicago when he went through Illinois. It was a city that he had always wanted to visit, but he was too anxious to get home, see his mother and father and put his plans into action. Black Sheet couldn't wait to meet the Caloosa Klan. He was able to gas up right outside of Chicago.

Once he was on the interstate, his only problem was hot food since he was able to gas up right outside of Chicago. He had a reserve in the car, but he didn't want to use it unless he had to. If he was lucky, he wouldn't run into the Klan. Southern Illinois was much like Mississippi—the stores, restaurants, and gas stations didn't cater much to Negros, and the Klan was deadly when it came to Negroes. He stopped at a gas station that sold sandwiches, but they refused to sell him anything. He was close to Cairo and hoped he could get hot food and gas there; otherwise, he would have to use a couple of the cans he had in his trunk for emergencies.

He saw his turnoff up ahead and tapped the brakes, slowing the car down for his exit. Ocean turned off the highway on to the road leading to Cairo, Illinois, the last town before leaving the state. He had survived the constant danger of war behind the lines while men were killed all around him. Now if he could just survive the war with the KKK at home.

He had left home a foolish boy of eighteen years old but was coming home a much wiser, discreet, perceptive, and even witty man. It looked so peaceful here compared to the war, but looks are deceiving—there was more hate for people of color behind the doors of these white people than he ever confronted in France and Germany. That was just war—a disagreement between countries. This was hate—pure unadulterated hate, an emotion energized by a difference in color and stimulated by a false sense of superiority. In that regard, southern Illinois was no better than Mississippi.

After hours of driving, just staring down the highway, and daydreaming about the future, he was feeling a little weary. He needed a hot meal, but trying to get food and fuel for a Negro traveling was no joke, especially when you were being refused even before you asked. Colored folks traveling down the highway had better carry their own food and fuel or risk going without—most restaurants would only serve whites. If he hadn't had those sandwiches and the fried chicken, he didn't know what he would have done.

He grimaced involuntarily, took his eyes off the road for just a second, and almost hit a light post just inside of Cairo, Illinois, still a long way from home. Hopefully he could find a hot meal here. He started to check that *Green Book* that his friend had slipped into his car but decided, *Well, I'm here now. I'll find out for myself.*

Now cruising slowly through Cairo, which was mostly eating supper this time of evening, he was looking for an open restaurant that might serve him some hot food. He knew it was unlikely, and he would have to eat a piece of the cold chicken that he had in the car, but he had to try. Maybe he could get some gas too. He still had four cans in the trunk of his car for emergencies, but he didn't want to use them unless he had to. Cairo, he knew, was as prejudiced against colored folks as any city in Mississippi. They had KKK and lynching parties where colored men were always the main attraction. He finally saw an open restaurant and gas station near the bridge to cross the Ohio River into Kentucky and pulled into a space right out front. The clerk was looking out the picture window, but the slowly disappearing sunrays were shining right in his face. The minute Oceans stepped out of the car, the clerk could see him, and he started shaking his head no and pointing to a sign in the window that said no Negros.

Now he wished he had followed his first mind and checked *The Negro Motorist Green Book*. At least he would know which roadside diners and gas stations would serve Negroes. Colored folks traveling down the highway carried their own food if they were smart. Most restaurants were only open to white travelers. Lucky for him that he had brought his own food, which had lost some of its freshness by now, and the three five-gallon cans of gas, and a sleeping bag. It seemed a shame that in 1945 Negroes needed a special guidebook showing safe places to stop when traveling the highways. Luckily, he had found a service station while still in Illinois that would serve Negroes and filled his tank so he hadn't had to use his extra gas. Running out of gas on a highway could lead to a life-or-death situation if you ran into the wrong white group.

An evil thought went through his mind, but he gritted his teeth and let it pass. As he approached the bridge into Kentucky, he looked at it with great apprehension. It was too narrow and just didn't look safe. The going would be slower from here on out. The towns along Highways 51 and 45 were notorious for speed traps. Plus, many had laws that banned Negros after dark. Suddenly, he felt kind of stupid; he had just gone through a war, and here he was worrying about speed traps and city ordinances that banned Negros after nightfall, but the danger was real. He had actually been safer in the German towns during the war than in the white towns in his own country.

He still had a long way to go. He'd be driving all day tomorrow through Kentucky, Tennessee, and then partway through Mississippi before he reached Caloosa.

The sunrays coming through his car window plus the bugs and insects having a merry time buzzing and singing and bouncing off his head pissed him off even more than being turned down for food.

He had one more night to go, and he needed rest badly. Ahead he saw a sign for a small town and decided to stop and see if he could rent a room for the night in the colored section. He slowed down for the drive through town. At first, he didn't see anything but white faces. Some—not used to seeing a black man in a nice car driving through town—looked at him and his car suspiciously, others with hostility.

He was just about to turn around and get the hell out of there when he spotted a colored face hurrying down the street. The colored man did a double take when he pulled up alongside and offered him a ride. There was a slight hesitation and a frown before he slid in.

"You visiting some body in town, brother, cause if you ain't, you need to get out of here fast cause there's trouble coming tonight."

"What kind of trouble you expecting?"

"Them Klu Klux Klan is on the warpath again. They gonna be out tonight raiding and killing black folks. This ain't no time for visiting."

"I'm not visiting. Just passing through, looking for a place to sleep tonight. I was just about to turn around when I saw you scurrying down the street. Thought there was no colored folks in town."

"We got plenty colored folks and plenty trouble," the man named Sidney insisted. "If I was you, I'd turn around and head right back to that highway."

"What's the problem? Why are you so scared? Is it past curfew or something?" Oceans said, laughing.

"It ain't funny. We expecting a visit from the KKK tonight. All the colored folks is taking refuge in they houses tonight."

"What kind of trouble you expecting?"

"Didn't you listen? The lynching kind. One of the Klansmen said a colored man looked at his daughter. That's always the excuse they use for lynching black men. They think we spend our days lusting after white women. Little do they know we got better things to do, and we got better women to do it with. They coming to teach all colored men and boys a lesson tonight."

"Maybe they need a lesson."

"They do, but who's going to give it to them? If we do it, the whole white community, which most of us work for, will be down on us. We'll lose lives, jobs, and money."

"Seems like you gonna lose lives anyway."

"Can't argue with that."

"So what you need is someone white to teach them, and then it can't be blamed on the colored folks."

"Yeah, but what white man's gonna go against their own? Ain't nobody that crazy."

"You may be surprised."

"You been warned. So you staying or going?"

"I'm staying if I can find a room. You know a place?"

"I can take you to Ms. Alberta's right around the corner. That's where the black baseball players stay when they're in town."

"Once I get settled, I'll contact my white friend and see if he can come here and give the Klan a taste of their own medicine."

"This ain't no joke, but yeah, that would be a blessing if it was possible, but I ain't holding my breath. Your white friend would have to have the wings of an angel to get here by tonight even if there was such a person. Come on. We here.

"Mrs. Alberta, this is Sergeant Oceans Tires. He's headed home from the army, and he needs a place to stay tonight."

"I got an extra room, but did you tell him about the Klan coming tonight?"

"I told him, but he still wants to stay. He thinks it's some kind of joke."

"Tell you the truth, Mrs. Alberta," he said whispering, "I think he hit his head fighting in that war, says he's got a white friend who can teach the Klan a lesson."

"Oh! You sure you want to stay, soldier? There's still time to go. These white folks don't care about you being no soldier—they kill you anyway."

"Do they just drive right down the middle of the street?"

"No, they like to tease us first. They set up a cross right in the middle of Main Street at the entrance to the colored section, and anybody they catch outside gets lynched. It's like a game to them."

"Only up to now there was no opposing team."

"We can't fight 'em. We done tried. Maybe when your friend gets here," he said winking, "from out of thin air, or is he coming down from the clouds? What do you think, Mrs. Alberta?"

"I think a puff of smoke or come out of a bottle like a genie."

"Tell you what, sarge, why don't you take this serious and stay off the street like the rest of us? You seem like a nice guy, and we wouldn't want to see nothing happen to you before you get home."

He watched the Klan as they set up a giant cross at the beginning of the colored section and torched it, igniting flames that leaped skyward. You could see it for blocks, maybe even miles. It was at least ten feet tall, rising menacingly into the night like a giant barn fire. Klansman were milling around the flickering flames in sinister-looking white sheets and menacing hoods with cruel eyes peeking out through huge clownlike eye holes. The whole scene was repugnant, appalling, ghoulish, terrifying, and kinda funny. Seeing the cross burning seemed to excite them. He didn't know whether it was the fire or the fact that they were embarking on another act of terror in the colored section, but whatever the motivation was, it lit them up as much as the cross. Now they were ready for whatever mischief they had planned.

It was time for Oceans to go into action. Members of the black community were clustered in the home of one of their leaders a few blocks away. They could see the huge cross burning from where they watched. They wanted to do something about this menace but knew what the penalty would be if they harmed these white men. Most of them either worked for the white man or depended on him in some way. Attacking the Klan would result in the small factory shutting down, day workers being laid off, field workers losing days. Restaurant workers, store clerks, janitors, and laborers would briefly lose their income, not to mention the reprisals by the Klan and even some seizure of property. Some men in the meeting were for attacking anyway, believing that it's never going to stop if they didn't do something.

"So what are we doing here!" screamed the most unlikely source, a young man barely out of his teens. "I could have watched them walking through the neighborhood burning and killing from my house."

"You're too young to understand," answered a man in his sixties.

"You think me and my friends haven't seen what's been happening? We're not taking it any longer."

"You better talk to your son, George, before he do something he'll be sorry for."

Suddenly a voice and a shot rang out. Thinking the raid had started, the black citizens prepared for the worse. But back at the cross, something unexpected was happening.

"What took you so long? I've been waiting for you."

"What? Who's that?"

Black Sheet made his entrance just as dramatically as the Klan. The sound of his rifle echoed again, giving the impression of a whole artillery barrage because of its proximity to his bullhorn. For a full minute, he had bullets hitting all around them, making them dance like they were at a high school prom. Then his voice echoed again through the bullhorn, sending shockwaves through the Klansmen who had never met resistance before. For a few seconds, they were paralyzed. His black sheet and hood looked ominous in the moonlight and weird with the stars twinkling like fireflies over his head.

"Look at yourself. You should be very proud. You come after dark. But that's not enough. You cover your faces with a hood and your body with a sheet so that no one knows who you are. You're ashamed of what you're doing? Why don't you be real men? Take off your hoods and let your neighbors know who you are. But you won't do that because you're all cowards. I challenge you. Take off your hoods and identify yourselves if you're so bad. Let your neighbors and these Negroes see you as you really are. You won't because you're nothing without your anonymity. Better still, turn around and go home. Live another day! Leave these people alone!"

"It couldn't be," Sidney reasoned, rejecting the idea right away. "It just couldn't be."

Then the voice came again, loud, clear, and definite. Oceans suddenly had a rush of confidence and conviction that was new to him. "If you stay here, you're going to die."

Then he frowned. Something new was happening to him. It was like demons had taken over his body. A disparaging question entered his mind. He suddenly questioned the absurdity of trying to reason with these cowardly men hiding behind white sheets with lynching on their minds. He tightened his grip on the rifle. Every muscle stood out clearly. He started shooting, and Klansmen started falling. Men and vehicles were being blown apart. Klansmen were running in every direction except through the Negro neighborhood.

When he finally stopped shooting, the intersection was littered with the bodies of men and wreckage. It looked like the aftermath of a combat incursion. After long minutes of silence, the colored people came out of hiding, curious to find out what the KKK had been shooting at and, to their amazement and shock, discovered a man in a black sheet and hood hurrying away from the scene, leaving behind dead and wounded Klansmen milling around aimlessly in shock, to stunned to know what happened.

One of the Klansmen was mumbling to himself, and as near as they could tell, a white man in a black sheet and hood had attacked them. "Must be the one we saw leaving," one of the black men reasoned, "but who was it?"

"The one he promised."

"What did you say, Sidney?"

"You wouldn't believe it," he grumbled, walking toward Mrs. Alberta's. "I don't believe it myself, and she won't either."

There was dead and wounded Klansmen lying around amidst the wreckage of their trucks and cars.

"Looks like they got a taste of their own medicine," snickered a man named Walter with no sympathy whatever.

"Help me!" one of the wounded Klansmen begged, his sheet red with his own blood.

"Did you hear anything?" an older man among the Negroes taunted.

"You talking about nerve. They came down here to lynch a few Negroes and got lynched themselves and expect us to help them. Far as I'm concerned, they can lay out there and die and rot right in the street."

The Negroes turned and, singing a catchy blues tune, went back home, leaving the Klansmen where they lay. Even though it was late, the news of the KKK bloodbath spread through the neighborhood with the speed of a flash of lighting.

Oceans wasn't proud of the killings, but felt it was just and had to be done. He was protecting the innocent Negro lives that would have been taken that night and made this town a better place for Negros to live. For that reason, he felt no guilt.

Mrs. Alberta met Sidney at the door. "I heard all of the shooting. How many did they kill?"

"None. The sergeant's friend showed up with that lesson he was talking about. Let's wake up the sarge and find out how he did it."

When they checked his room, they found him there sound asleep.

"Sergeant! Sergeant!" Mrs. Alberta shouted excitedly. "Wake up! Wake up! You did it. We don't know how, but you did it! The Klan got a taste of their own medicine. They got just what was coming to them. And they got it from a white man."

"Yeah," Sidney agreed calmly. "They're bleeding like pigs under their own cross all over the corner."

Oceans feigned just waking up. "Wha-what's happening?" he mumbled indistinctly and yawned.

"Didn't you hear me? Just what you said," Sidney answered in a strong calm voice. "Some white guy showed up and attacked the Klan just like you said he would."

"So no Negroes were hurt or killed?"

"They didn't even get past the corner."

"Well, I'm glad," he said stretching, "but I didn't say it would happen. I said it would be good if it did. So what are you gonna do now?"

"We just gonna wait and see what the white folks gonna do."

It was the worst humiliation the Klan had ever suffered. For the city itself, it was a terrible tragedy, and a few of the prominent citizens were struggling with the loss of loved ones.

When Oceans drove out the next morning, the sheriff and his deputies were questioning Sidney and his neighbors about the previous night's events.

It wasn't going to be a good day weather-wise. Dark clouds covered the sky. It looked like a storm was brewing. After about ten miles, he could see the rain coming toward him from the south in sheets, and it was heavy. He met it head on at fifty miles an hour. It was like someone was throwing buckets of water against his windshield. He gripped the wheel with both hands and plowed on through. It was just one of those quick summer storms. It didn't last long. He was soon out of Kentucky and into Tennessee.

WHAT LIES AHEAD DOWN THE ROAD?

All of the restaurants along the highway had refused to serve him. They even looked at him and his car suspiciously like they thought he may have stolen it. He had stopped twice, the first time at a little restaurant just off the highway for a sit-down meal. The place wasn't crowded. In fact, it was almost empty. It was about 11:00 p.m.; there were only a couple of cars in the lot, and he felt sure a soldier in uniform coming home from the war, even a black one, would be served. But they just ignored him. Didn't even have the courtesy to say, "We don't serve colored people." Just let him sit there until, disgusted, he got up and walked out.

Around one o'clock, he decided to try again, this time at a little roadside diner for a sandwich to go. They were more courteous. They came right out and said, "We don't serve no niggers."

He didn't even take offense. "Do you serve soldiers?" he asked politely.

Before he could answer, an older man walked up. "Is there a problem, Jedadia?" he asked the waiter.

"I told him we don't serve his kind, but he wants to know if we serve soldiers." It seemed the waiter was confused. He knew he couldn't serve colored folks, but he didn't know about soldiers, and this man was both.

The owner just looked at him with disgust, shaking his head. Finally, he turned to Oceans, "Go around to the back, and we'll hand you something out the back door."

After all, he was in the south. What did he expect? "Tell you what," Oceans answered, "why don't you serve it to your next white customer or, better still, stick it up your goddamn hunky ass."

"Now see here, nigger, there's no call for that."

"See there," he heard the owner say as he walked to his car, "you can't be nice to them."

Oceans had an impulse to break the front window as he walked out but decided that would do more harm than good.

Grabbing a cold piece of chicken and taking a big bite, he thought of home and home cooking. He could almost smell the ham, hot crispy fried chicken, biscuits, grits, bacon, and eggs on his mother's breakfast table. The thought was driving him insane.

He thought he would never get out of Tennessee. He still had miles to go to reach the Mississippi border. The sway of the car lulled him into a daydream about his childhood in Caloosa, Mississippi. This was a place he thought he'd never come back to once he got out. Now, here he was headed back there at a faster speed than when he left. And looking forward to it.

A sudden premonition brought him out of his reverie, or was it a sound? He couldn't be sure. Out there on the highway at night, the sound carried. Then a muffled scream seemed to reach his ears. A short distance ahead, he saw some trucks pulled over to the side of the highway and flames from a fire just inside the trees. A loud chilling scream penetrated the silence, and Oceans involuntarily stepped on the brake and was pulling over to the side before he realized what he was doing.

Not again! his mind shrieked. *It can't be.* He was compelled to investigate.

An hour earlier, four Klansmen and the grand dragon of the region were drinking. They were half-drunk and bored when a colored man walked past after working late cleaning up the restaurant where he worked. Seeing him, one of them remarked, "You see what I see? Let's have some fun. Let's lynch this nigger."

"For what?"

"For fun, what else?"

"Yeah, Charley, you still got that barbed wire in the back of your truck. Now that would make a terrible mess. Come on. Let's do it."

Night was a dangerous time for Negroes in most southern towns. If it wasn't curfews or hate, it was just plain meanness. Cowardly acts by white mobs were commonplace, and most Negroes knew it and tried to stay off the streets at night. There were few, if any, cases of a Negro being attacked by a single white male.

Oceans took his rifle and had a deep breath, which he slowly exhaled, and walked to the edge of the woods where he witnessed another gruesome sight. White men in KKK garb and one in regular clothes had stripped a black man and wrapped him in barbed wire, and the one in civilian clothing was waving a long sharp knife over his genitals, smiling as he prepared to castrate him. *Not again,* his internal voice screamed. *What is it with white men that they have to maim and kill black men even though black men are considered inferior? Maybe it's themselves that they see as mediocre.*

He was so enraged that he just started shooting. Three men fell before the others disappeared back into the trees. He could hear them running over the echo of the rifle. One of the wounded men was struggling to get up.

"Get that wire off him!" Oceans demanded in his best white voice.

"I can't. I'm hurt. You shot me."

"Get that wire off him," Oceans urged, "or I'll shoot you again and wrap you in it."

"You're a white man. Why are you taking this nigger's side over me?"

Oceans shot again but not to kill even though he deserved it.

"Please! Please! Don't shoot again. I don't want to die."

"He doesn't want to die either. Never mind. I'll just kill you and take the wire off myself. No! No! Please! I'm doing it."

The black man was just repeating, "Thank you, Jesus! Thank you, Jesus!"

Once he got the wire off, Oceans told the black man, "Now wrap him in it."

"No! No. You can't wrap me in it. You promised."

"Well, I lied. Wrap him up."

"With pleasure," the former victim eagerly agreed. "An eye for an eye. Never thought I'd agree to that."

"Okay, now start running after your friends," Oceans ordered.

"I can't. I can't run in this wire."

"Then die in it."

The Klansman took off limping through the woods with the wire flapping behind him.

"Come on quick!" Oceans yelled to the colored man who was already running toward him. When they got to the highway, Oceans started shooting up the trucks except for the first one. That's when the black man got a good look at him.

"You're black," he said surprised.

"I know," Oceans replied, getting in his car. "Let's get the hell out of here. Take that first truck and ditch it somewhere. Good luck."

"Thanks. I'll never forget you!" the grateful victim yelled driving away.

ASSAULT ON SIMMONS

Wesley Simmons was the epitome of racism in a land where deep embedded racism ran rampant. Even though Negroes had been free almost one hundred years, in his mind and actions they were still in bondage, and he wanted them to see themselves in that light too. He was constantly trying to accelerate the existing Jim Crow laws to eliminate what little freedom the Negro felt they still had. It wasn't enough for them to be treated like they were less than white people. He wanted them to feel like less than white people, but he could only do so much as grand dragon. He could terrorize, but that wasn't enough. He wanted to make and enforce policies.

When he said he wanted to be mayor, everybody laughed. His beliefs were so extreme that they knew he could never be elected. He opened his campaign by accusing all Negroes of being thieves, rapist, killers as well as being lazy, deceitful, conniving, sneaky, dishonest, and cunning. Then to everybody's surprise, he won, and the laughter became despair then agony then resignation.

His greatest passion was hate for colored people. His greatest objective was making things as bad as possible for them by strengthening the already-stringent policies against them. His advisers were all known members of the KKK. He immediately added new and more rigorous policies. There was a 7:00 p.m. curfew for all Negroes. They could no longer own property. Their already-low wages were cut. The penalties for breaking laws were increased. This was just one more atrocity committed against the colored population during the Jim Crow era.

The colored people fought back in the only way they could. They stopped showing up for work, cut down on the quality of their work when they did show up, stopped shopping at the chain stores like Woolworths, Kroger, and Piggly Wiggly. Business was suffering. Private homeowners were complaining about domestic workers who either didn't show up or did shoddy work.

Fruit were rotting in the orchards. Cotton, wheat, and cornfields went unpicked, and white tempers started to rise. The new policies had been turned against them. As long as it only hurt the Negro, it was acceptable. Now even some of the Klan members thought Simmons had gone too far. But he wouldn't listen. He doubled down on the negativity, causing the city to suffer even more.

He called his top man into his office whom he referred to as his enforcer and gave him a special assignment. "It's come to my attention that Reverend Nathan Turner has been encouraging his members to rebel against all Jim Crow laws and the new policies that I've established. Take four men out to his house and teach him a lesson."

"Do you want us to lynch him?"

"Don't kill him, just give him a good beating, burn his house down, and warn him that if he doesn't stop the defiance, something could happen to his family.

Unknown to him his plan, was heard by a black man working in the courthouse. He couldn't believe his ears. He knew the grand dragon was evil, but to grab a man of God, beat him, burn his house, and threaten his family was unthinkable. He had to stop him, and he planned to do just that. He warned Reverend Turner, but the whole idea was so despicable that the reverend didn't believe it. He was severely beaten, and his house was torched not long afterward.

On his way home a few days later, Wesley Simmons was attacked and beaten to within an inch of his life, saved only because a group of whites returning from deer hunting came upon the scene, stopped the assault, captured his assailant, and lynched him.

THE DAY AFTER

Oceans was ecstatic after stopping two assaults of colored men. Until now he didn't know how active the Klan was along the highways at night. Truth was it was unsafe for colored people to be out late at night in these towns that bordered the highways, drivers as well as pedestrians.

Well, I'd better get my mind back on driving. This daydreaming could get a fellow killed, and I didn't live through four years of war to come home and get killed in a car accident.

Early the next morning, he started to see familiar landmarks. He had crossed Tennessee into Mississippi. He only had about 150 miles to go.

The sun was just coming up over the trees in the east, and he could see the dew shining on the grass out of his driver's side window. The last of the night sounds were fading, the frogs, the night birds, the screech owls, the night hawks, the nightingales, even the whippoorwills were all heading for the nest after a long night of hunting and scavenging. He didn't realize how much he had missed these sounds until now. This was the last stretch of highway before reaching the outskirts of Caloosa, Mississippi. Thirty minutes later, he crossed the county line entering the outskirts of Caloosa.

He passed the Welcome Motel on Center Street with the "No Colored" sign in the window. A mile or so later, he passed the Kroger grocery store on Pearl Street and, a few blocks later, its only competition, the Piggly Wiggly grocery store. Once he crossed the railroad tracks, he was home.

Not much had changed in five years. The fields on the side of the highway were white with cotton buds, and the field workers had beaten daylight to the fields and were already out picking. He pulled the visor down to block the sun, which was reflecting off the hood of his car and shining directly into his tired red eyes. He slowed his car to avoid the coming speed trap that his father had cursed so many times. Nothing had changed. Speed traps were still one of the best sources of revenue in this part of Mississippi. The speed limit suddenly changed from fifty miles per hour to twenty-five miles per hour, catching anyone unfamiliar with the trap completely unaware. But he was already cruising at twenty miles per hour. He had an urge to wave at the troopers in the patrol car sitting back out of sight in the trees near the highway, but he dismissed it. It didn't pay for a black man to get too cocky. They could always make up a charge to arrest him, and a black man didn't have a chance in a Jim Crow court. Instead, he concentrated on keeping his speed below twenty-five miles per hour. He reached up and gave the dashboard of his new Chevy a loving pat.

Well, it was new only to him, but he was still proud of his 1940 Chevy sedan. It was his first car bought and paid for with some of the back money grudgingly given to him by the army after over four years missing in action. He knew he had been badly overcharged for the car, but what black man was foolish enough to expect a fair deal in 1945?

He made a right turn on to Fourth Street and again marveled at the beautiful pre–Civil War homes (antebellum) in this white stretch of Fourth Street. Then he crossed the tracks, leaving the paved white side of Fourth Street and entering the colored section and the gravel roads, dry and dusty from lack of rain and lack of pavement. Black neighborhoods were still being neglected by the white power structure. But he was proud to see that many of the black homeowners were showing pride in their homes by planting flowers, painting, and putting in their own paved sidewalks and driveways. Black labor was responsible for most of the labor work in the city anyway.

Still in full uniform, he brushed a little dirt off of the lapels. He couldn't do anything about the wrinkles. He leaned closer to the window and stared out without emotion at the half-dressed children running barefoot in the yards.

Now that he was close to home, he could barely wait to see his mother and father and his friends. He didn't even know if his friends were still around after all of these years. Funny that he hadn't really thought about them in the last few years as close as they had been. The Akan Royals, they had called themselves as a tribute to Osei Obiri's native language of Akan. It would be good to see them again.

After all these years, he thought to himself, *things look the same.* He made a right turn off Fourth onto Main Street. *How can I stay here now that I've seen London, New York, and Chicago?* He had visited these cities before coming home. Yet this was his hometown with all of its flaws. If it was going to change, the people had to change it. He couldn't wait to see the surprised look on his family's faces who didn't know he was arriving home today. His mother would cry. His father would show little visible emotion, but if you looked closely, you could see the held-back tears glistening in his eyes.

CHAPTER 4

Home At Last

It was a struggle, but Oceans overcame his negative thoughts, changed his whole demeanor, dismissed his doubts and misgivings, and tried to see his hometown as what it could be without the vast restrictions put on the lives of Negroes. Still, he couldn't ignore what it was. His plan was to try to diminish, minimize, or eliminate the influence of the KKK and repeal the demoralizing Jim Crow laws if only in his town. It wouldn't be an easy task. People would die. White people.

Those thoughts dominated his mind, and he focused on his plan to stimulate change. The most immediate fear for colored folks, especially colored men, was the KKK who took pleasure in lynching black men for little or no reason. He remembered hearing as a boy about a black man dragged out of his house and lynched after he accidentally bumped into a white man and knocked him off the sidewalk. Later, it was learned that the incident never happened.

As a child, Oceans had been unpredictable, constantly devising little schemes to show his disrespect for white authority, continually picking fights with the young white boys his age, and demonstrating reckless behavior in public. He soon had a reputation as a troublemaker. His parents blamed his behavior on the influence of Osei Obiri before he was killed and the effect his death had on Oceans. He never got over the terrible way Obiri died. Many of his parents' friends believed it was only by the grace of God that Oceans wasn't lynched. Even his parents were afraid for him and glad to see him leave for the army although by that time he had calmed down a little.

Now, he was back with a carefully planned fighting agenda. This time, no more reckless public behavior. Everything he did would be covert. Outwardly, he would be a model, conforming young colored man. This Ocean would make no waves.

MOMMY B

He made a right turn onto Mulberry Street. Mommy B was sitting on the porch at the corner house, rocking slowly in that same old rocking chair and dipping her snuff. It was just like he had left yesterday. He pulled over and got out of the car. He just wanted to say hello and give her a hug.

"Oceans! My God it's good to see you, but I wish you hadn't come home on this sad day."

"What happened, Momma B? What's wrong?"

"It's your friend Ben, lynched down on Main Street."

"But why, Mommy B?"

"Yesterday he attacked and beat up Wesley Simmons."

Oceans was stunned, left speechless, but Momma B saw something in his eyes, leaned precariously out of her chair, grabbed him, and said, "Don't do anything crazy, son."

He pushed her away gently and ran off the porch.

The clock had stopped here in Caloosa. Nothing had changed. The memories came flooding back. He thought about his friend Osei Obiri lynched because he used the white bathroom and attacked Wesley Simmons, a grand dragon in the Klan. Now his friend Ben had met the same fate.

Mommy B had done her best to keep him out of trouble, and he probably owed his life to her. Now she was worried about him doing something crazy again. He remembered vividly the day he came close to killing the mayor's son. As far back as he could remember, white men and boys had prowled the colored neighborhoods looking for unsuspecting colored women and girls to proposition, harass, and even rape. Some even had the audacity to approach black men and solicit them to help find a "clean" black woman or girl. To his knowledge, no white man had ever been killed for this behavior, but they should have been.

His thoughts turned to the day he and his friends had witnessed such an action. He and his three best friends, Kenny, John, and Ben, were walking down the street after school when they heard a vehicle screech to a stop behind them.

It was around 2:15 p.m., when he was fourteen years old, on a hot sticky day in June with hardly any wind blowing. The temperature was 100 degrees in the sparse shade that the oak trees gave out and even hotter inside the houses along Mulberry Street. People were sitting on the front porches on both sides of the street trying to catch whatever breeze they could. Oceans and his best friends, John, Kenny, and Ben, were hurrying away from school, glad to be off for the summer when they heard a disturbance behind them. Even though the school itself was in a swampy, muddy field, this street was paved and had sidewalks.

Mulberry was one of the few streets in the colored neighborhood that had a sidewalk, and it was buckling from the heat. He figured that the only reason the street was paved and had a sidewalk in the first place was because a few white people lived on it.

It was the horn blowing in this quiet neighborhood and the sudden scream that captured their attention. Then the catcalls started. They turned around to see what was happening and saw a pickup truck pull up on the sidewalk. Three young white punks, obviously high on moonshine and looking for young black girls, jumped out and grabbed two young colored girls walking home from school. Screaming, the girls fought back frantically.

"This little nigger bitch is feisty as hell!" one of the boys jeered. "Come on, girl. You know you want it," he said and slapped her across the face. "Get your black ass in the truck."

Oceans turned and ran back, viciously attacking the white boys as they tried to wrestle the young girls into the bed of the truck. The unexpected attack caught the boys by surprise, and before they could recover, his friends had joined the fracas. Oceans straddled the one who appeared to be the leader and punched him repeatedly while talking to him, "You. Can't. Come. Into. Our. Neighborhood. And. Assault. Our. Girls. Like. We. Ain't. Nothing. I'll. Kill. Your. Punk. Ass."

The idea that they had the audacity to come into the colored neighborhood to snatch young girls enraged him to the point of losing all reason. He was in a killing rage and had temporally lost all sense of reasoning. The nerve of them bypassing the white girls in their neighborhood to come to their neighborhood to humiliate and dishonor their black girls.

"That's enough, boy," a voice said from the side.

"Oceans! Let him up before you kill him," the voice persisted. A little old lady with a limp and a cane had hobbled out of a yard that looked like a flower garden with roses and tulips and looked down at the boy Oceans was beating. "Let him up before you kill him," she commanded again.

"But he was going to rape one of our girls."

"I know what he was doing, but listen to Momma B. Let him up.

"Is that you Jeb Wesley Simmons, Jr.?" she questioned as she pulled Oceans off of him. "I know you and your father too. He just gave you that truck and you driving around here drunk as a skunk hassling people.

"You girls, run on home," she said. "Get away from here! You're safe now.

"I saw you trying to abduct the girls, and that's a crime that even white boys can go to jail for. Also, you been drinking. If you don't get away from here now, I'm going to tell your father you were drunk and out of order, and you know he listens to Momma B cause I raised him," she declared. "If he knew you were driving drunk, your father would take that truck away from you." She knew of course that they wouldn't be punished for trying to abduct two black girls. Like the apple, nuts didn't fall to far from the tree. His father wouldn't be mad. He'd be proud, but driving drunk was a different story.

"And you, Oceans, your mother raised you better than this, and I know your father wouldn't like it."

After the boys in the truck drove away, she turned back to Oceans. "You did the right thing, boy, trying to save those girls. They would have raped them for sure. But you don't want to get into it with him," she said. "His father is a grand dragon in the KKK. You gave him a good whipping, one he won't soon forget, and that was enough. You've got to be smarter than they are." She smiled. "They don't like that."

"I know, Momma B," Oceans responded. "I just got so mad."

"I know you felt like killing him, but that wouldn't have solved anything, just made you and your family more trouble. The apple don't fall to far from the tree. His father is just like him. He just doesn't know it yet. If you've got to fight back, find a way to do it without them knowing it's you."

As she started to turn back to her house, Oceans heard her grunt.

"Are you all right, Momma B?"

"My rheumatism is acting up a little bit, but don't worry about me. I've had worse. Now go on home, boy, and think about what I just said."

Momma B was over eighty years old, and she had witnessed many white atrocities against colored people. She didn't want to see this boy become a victim. He was smart but impulsive and aggressive, and when the change came, and it would come, they would need men like him.

"If you have to fight, find a way to do it without them knowing it's you," she had said. The thought had lain dormant in his mind all of these years. Now he had a way to hide his identity, but he couldn't tell her.

BEN'S LYNCHING

He could see the crowd milling around from over a block away. He tried to prepare his head, his heart, his mind for what he was about to see, but it was impossible. He would never be ready for this. His first glimpse of the horrific sight was devastating, and he almost ran his car off the road and into the crowd. He just wasn't prepared for the disfiguring they had done to his friend.

He saw his other childhood friend, John Henry, moving around aimlessly, seemingly broken beyond repair. He got out of his car and walked toward the front. His intention was to find out from John Henry what had caused this to happen, but when he got close to him and got a closer look at Ben, the question didn't seem important. After all the killing and maiming he had seen and done in the war and knowing that Mississippi was just another war zone for blacks, he didn't think anything could surprise him. But the thing he saw hanging from a limb in those trees looked like it had been blown to bits in a minefield. One arm was off; the other was missing. Brains were hanging out of the head across the face, which was completely disfigured. What was left of his face was etched in pain, and Oceans could imagine that wherever he was now in death, his friend was feeling nothing but relief. Both legs were so twisted that they no longer looked like legs, and what was left of the victim had been set on fire. Its own mother wouldn't have recognized it. Oceans knew he didn't.

It was obvious from the scrapes and dismemberment that he had been dragged behind a car for blocks before he was strung up on this willow tree. Oceans just hoped Ben wasn't alive when he was dragged, but the agony on his face showed that he might have been.

The sunlight and drooping limbs of the weeping willow tree cast an eerie shadow over the body as it gently swung on the rope. Flies buzzed all around the corpse and little groups of gnats swarmed, forcing the wild-eyed spectators to constantly fan and swat them away. Blood was splattered as far as five feet away. This had been a public lynching, and Ben had suffered greatly.

The morning was hot and humid. The squirrels were active, running up and down nearby trees and limbs, chasing each other on the ground. It was just another summer day for them. Quite unaware of the human tragedy around them, they continued to play. Birds were chirping, singing, and flying unperturbed while Oceans stood there under the same trees, the same sky trying to understand it all. He should have been horrified, but he had seen so much death in the war that all he could feel was vengeful.

It was the needlessness of his death that got to him the most, the feeling of hopelessness he must have felt in his last moments. To be killed just because he was black, it just wasn't fair. That human beings could have so much hate that they could do such a thing to someone was beyond belief. But the Klan wasn't human. They were a pack of animals—the only difference being that they walked on two legs and wore clothes.

Oceans had seen this stand of trees a million times as a boy. He and his friends had played there together as boys. Now, if possible, he was even more determined to end the reign of these ruthless beasts in Caloosa. Ben was his friend, but he wasn't the only reason for his fight against the Klan and the Jim Crow laws. There was Obiri, the loss of confidence, ambition, and the feeling of inferiority in the Negro community but especially the terror. He vowed to show them that he could be just as savage to them as they were to Ben and other lynch victims. He would create the same kind of terror in their neighborhoods as they had created in his although he recognized that all white folks were not as bad as the Klan.

The area leading up to the lynch site was the most public spot they could find right on Main Street, not far from the police station and the courthouse. So the police had known it was happening—may have even been in on it. There were cigarette butts, trash, and even food wrappers around the benches that were located near the area. Even a couple of broken chairs and a blankets were thrown on the grass near the trees. Just a pleasant outing for everyone except the victim. Scraps of clothing were scattered everywhere, and his shoes were lying on the edge of the clearing. One of them had blood inside and on the toe. There were footprints all around the area, indicating that at least ten or twelve people took part in the violence or at least watched it.

The whole scene looked like something out of a war zone, and in a way it was even though this was Caloosa, his hometown. The Germans and the KKK had a lot in common. In his stupor, he had forgotten about John Henry. When he finally tore his eyes away from Ben, John was staring at him like he was seeing a ghost. His face reflected surprise, disbelief, happiness, and sadness. Like two zombies, they embraced each other.

"Thought you was dead," John Henry said.

"That's what the army thought until a few months ago," Oceans answered, his eyes turning back toward the trees. The KKK had been poetic in picking the weeping willow tree to showcase this grotesque scene of savagery.

"You shouldn't have come back, O. You should have stayed away."

"I couldn't. This is my home. My family and friends are here."

"Yeah, and if we don't get out now, we'll never leave. If you don't believe me, look at Ben. If he had left, he wouldn't be where he is now. I'm getting out, O. There's nothing left here for me. I don't want to end up like Ben. I guess his own mother wouldn't recognize him now." John started finally breaking down.

As he stood there looking, his fingers closed into fist so tight that they ached. He had trouble breathing. His eyelids tightened to help block out the tears; his shoulders locked and cramped. His knees tried to buckle. He tried to find words in his mind to explain this, but they just wouldn't come. His thoughts were scattered and confused. This was war, and he wanted to kill somebody. The Germans, the KKK, what was the difference? He knew he had to do something, and maybe killing was the answer. If some Klan members die, maybe they'll stop killing.

John Henry broke into his thoughts. "I'm taking the first freight out of here going north today. I'm not spending another night in this goddamn town."

"I understand how you feel, but you can't leave now. At least stay until after we bury Ben."

"You just don't know," John cried. "You just don't know. You haven't been here. It's gotten even worse since the war ended." John was so distraught that Oceans could not make sense of what he was saying. He was blabbering something about the Klan. "The Klan," he kept mumbling. "The Klan."

"Why? Come on, John, get yourself together. Talk to me."

"Ben heard Wesley Simmons making plans to lynch a black man just for the hell of it. He waited for Wesley near his office and attacked him. He was going to kill him, but some white men came along and stopped him. They brought him out here and lynched him. He didn't have a chance. His mother sent me to look for him this morning. I hate to have to tell her this."

Being black in the South was a curse. Being black anywhere was a curse. "I don't blame you for getting out, but, John, where will you go?"

"I've got a cousin in Detroit. It's not perfect, but it is better than this. There's no lynching. They've got other problems."

"Come on. Let's cut him down, "Oceans urged. "That's the least we can do."

"I know this sounds bad, O, but I can't touch him, not the way he looks. That's not even Ben anymore."

"It's still Ben, and we can't leave him hanging here. We owe him that much for old times' sake. If I cut him down, will you help me put him in the back of your truck and take him to the funeral home? His mother shouldn't see him looking like this."

"I'm sorry, Oceans, I just wasn't thinking. But, Oceans, how we gonna pick him up? He's falling apart," John half whispered, his mouth trembling.

"Take it easy, John. I've got a blanket in my car. We can wrap him up in that."

During the war, Oceans had witnessed and participated in many gruesome scenes and thought he had become immune to this type of violence, but nothing prepares you for the violent death of a friend especially when they die like this. In the war, he had killed without feeling or mercy because the Germans were his country's enemies, but this was pure hate. This was war albeit a different kind of war, but war nevertheless.

Walking up to that tree, Oceans could almost feel the violence still present. Although the lynching was long over, he was hard put to hold back the rage. He tried not to imagine the suffering that his friend had endured. Better times tried to invade his thoughts as he approached Ben's body, but the sight before him blocked them out, and they were replaced by thoughts of violence. He looked up at his friend, squeezed his eyes shut, trying unsuccessfully to hold back the tears, and just groaned. He had seen death, but nothing like this. This disfigured mess wasn't Ben. Ben was high spirited, outgoing, happy-go-lucky, full of life. Somebody would pay soon. The Klan had to die. But even in his grief, he knew that it wouldn't be easy to kill the Klan, yet he could paralyze the part of the body that extended into Caloosa.

Finally, he stopped fighting and let the tears flow freely. His fight was with the Klan, not the tears. He spread the blanket under the tree and reached up to cut the rope.

"Leave him up there," a white bystander demanded when Oceans raised the knife to cut the rope. He ignored the command and started to cut. "What's wrong, nigger? Are you deaf? Leave him hanging there."

"I have a better idea. You take him down."

"Well, what do you know, Bigelow?" another white bystander snarled. "We got us one of them smart niggers here."

Without another word, Oceans walked over and grabbed him in the collar then pushed him up against the tree right under Ben. Holding out his knife, he said, "Now you cut him down, or I'm going to cut you up!"

"Are you crazy, nigger?"

"Get him down quick, or you're going to find out."

"Okay! Okay, I'll get him down. Just take it easy with that knife."

"I should put you up there with him. Now get him down and lay him on this blanket."

"You gonna let this nigger do this to me, Marty?"

"What can I do? There's only two of us."

By the time they got him on the blanket, they were covered with blood. The crowd of black bystanders had become agitated at the sight of the broken body lying on the blanket, and it was inciting them to violence toward the two white spectators. Oceans was afraid harming them would lead to more violence that could spread into the nearby colored community, so he tried to calm the crowd.

"Forget about them. This is not the time. Help me get Ben's body into the bed of the truck.

"Pull the truck up, John," he called, ignoring the gapers. Turning slowly and deliberately to face the two bigots, Oceans stared at them for a moment and then spoke to them. They started to back away then turned and walked away, promising meekly that there would be another day.

Two black men in overalls walked up, patted Oceans on the back, and said, "Come on, soldier, we'll help."

"We'll take him to Bruce Funeral Home, then I'll follow you to Ben's house," Oceans said to John as he turned toward his car. "Well, the three of us are together again for the last time. Never, when we were growing up, could I have imagined that things could end up like this," Oceans reflected. *Since I've been away, things have gotten worse—if that's possible,* he thought to himself. *Something has to be done about the Klan soon. It's too late for Ben, but maybe I can save some others.*

Bruce sent his sons out to get Ben's body, and even they were surprised at the shape it was in. Now Oceans and John had the dreaded duty of telling his parents.

Oceans turned into Ben's yard behind John Henry. The air was still, not even a whisper of a breeze. Cold sweat dampened his face and underarms. He looked up at the cloudless sky. The sunrays were blinding. Not even the birds were flying as if out of respect for this solemn occasion. John Henry drove his truck right up to the porch where Ben's mother and father were sitting, and for a few seconds that seemed like minutes, time stopped.

His parents didn't move, just sat there staring and trying to compose themselves before they confronted the inevitable news. Slowly they stood and came off the front porch. Ben's father limped, showing the effects of the beating he had taken the night before. Oceans could tell by their body language that they were expecting the worst and could only regret that he and John Henry, Ben's best friends, were the ones bringing them the news.

He stepped out of his car into the hot still air. His eyes burned from holding back the tears. It felt like a dream, but this was for real. His hands were trembling. His heart was beating faster. A strange oppressiveness came down on Oceans as he watched Ben's parents stop at the truck bed.

"We took him straight to the funeral home," Oceans said, walking over. He just stood there silently and watched as Mr. Wolfe's eyes reached flood stage and tears overflowed to his cheeks and dripped off his chin on to his chest.

The silence was broken by the bloodcurdling scream of Ben's mother as she broke down and fell to her knees. It chilled his heart.

"Mrs. Wolfe," Oceans called, but she was too distraught to respond. He repeated her name several times before she heard him. Then she looked up. "Is there anything we can do?" The tragic loss in her eyes haunted him.

He looked past Ben's parents to a spot somewhere in the future, maybe even in Mississippi, somewhere in the future where you couldn't just kill and maim a black man with no consequence. There was bitterness in his thoughts, and the pain he felt was almost unbearable. He could just imagine how they must feel after losing their son in such a tragic way. His heart went out to them.

Memories of their childhood came flooding back. He tried, but he couldn't stop the memories. They just kept coming. He had to do something. Everything in this city was stacked against colored people. No matter how smart they were, only menial jobs and menial education were available to them.

Hearing Ben's mother scream again brought him out of his reverie and back to reality. Ben's mother, father, and even John were crying, but he couldn't get another tear past the fury and frustration. He made a silent vow to himself to never stop until he reached his goal. "It's too late for you, Ben," he said to the sky, "but not for the rest of us. I'm gonna turn a lot of white sheets red."

This was the worst homecoming that he could have imagined.

CHAPTER 5

My House At Last

Oceans made his turn onto Third Street and saw the steeple on the top of Third Street Baptist Church in the middle of the block, and it brought to mind one of the stupid pranks he had pulled as a child. It resulted in a public whipping by his father and an apology to the whole church congregation. On a dare, he climbed to the roof and draped the pastor's robe over the steeple. His mother and father were so mad and embarrassed that they stayed away from church a full month until the pastor and a few of the elders came by the house and begged them to come back.

There used to be a hitch rail for horses in front of the church right under that big walnut tree for those members who lived on farms and didn't have cars or trucks. It was still there when he left. Now he noticed that it was gone. As a child, he and his friends would swing on that hitching rail, and the walnut tree was the source of a lot of walnut missiles that the kids threw or shot with a slingshot at each other. All of the boys had slingshots because all it took was an old inner tube and a small V-shaped tree branch, and you could make it yourself. They had to be inventive and make their own playthings because there was no money to spare to buy them, and even if they had had the money, they wouldn't let colored folks in Woolworths to spend it.

One time he and his friends sneaked in to buy Dubble Bubble gum, and the clerk refused to sell it to them, but Oceans used his talent to throw his voice and, seeing the manager walking away behind the clerk, said, "Give them two apiece" in the manager's voice. The clerk looked back where the voice came from and saw the manager walking away and said okay and gave them each two pieces of bubble gum.

It's funny the things you think about at a time like this. They were, as Indians would say, blood brothers, and Oceans felt that some of his blood had been spilled that day. He had three good friends. Now one of them was dead. Lynched.

He was determined to stop the Klan in Caloosa! The only possible way was to defrock and exposé the individuals for what and who they were. They are basically thugs hiding behind white sheets and hoods by night and white faces and respectability by day. They were neighbors, pretend friends, teachers, lawyers, doctors, mayors, sheriffs, deputy sheriffs, and even pastors but all racist. They were controlling the lives of colored people through Jim Crow laws, violence, and threats of violence. Those same threats applied to whites too. If they thought it didn't apply to whites, just do something for blacks that's against the rules.

Finally, he was turning on his block. He waved to the neighbors that he passed doing various projects in the front yards, and they waved back and smiled. A slight smile came to his lips because he knew that they didn't know who he was, not from this distance and driving a strange car, but that was the friendly way of the South. People spoke whether they knew you or not.

Oceans turned on to the long bumpy lane leading up to his parents' house. The fields on both sides of the lane were lush with corn. Sunflowers, some as tall as eight feet, grew wild alongside of the lane. That familiar aroma unique only to the sunflower permeated the hot air and made it even stuffier. He could tell that today was going to be hotter than usual. Ahead of him and on the left, he could see a few cows and goats grazing contently. In his rearview mirror, he could see a dust cloud billowing behind him. He slowed down. His mother wouldn't be happy if the wind blew the dust onto her clean clothes hanging on the line. As he turned into the yard, chickens scattered getting out of the way then immediately reoccupied the vacated space. He wondered how his mother and father, one an educator and principal of the local black school the other educated but working as the school janitor at the white school, still had the time and energy to work a farm. As his father had often said, "You do what you have to do and keep the faith." Oceans had his doubts.

The house sat on ten acres of land—not a big farm by Mississippi standards, but productive. Way over in the corner of the yard was a pigpen with a boar, male pig for breeding, and a sow, a female pig, with piglets. A thriving garden was growing behind a fence not too far away. He stopped the car beside his father's truck, next to the storage shed.

His mother heard the car coming and ran out of the door. He was out of the car and running to embrace her even before the car came to a complete stop.

"I knew you would be coming today," she said between sobs. "I even told your father, and I fixed your favorite supper, fried chicken, collard greens, candied sweet potatoes, okra, cornbread, and I made you a big peach cobbler, but I'm getting ahead of myself. Your breakfast is ready. Come on in and eat."

"I never could fool you, Mubba. You know me too well."

His father, a six-foot-two muscular slow-talking man of forty-five years old, stepped off the porch and grabbed him in a bear hug. As close as they were, this was something his father had never done. In all of Oceans's twenty-three years, his father had never hugged him like this. "I'm just so glad to have you home and safe, son," he said, holding back the tears. "When we heard you were missing in action, well, you're here now that's all that matters." He had never seen his father this emotional. "Your Uncle Bubba just left. He told us about Ben."

"I know," Oceans answered. "I just helped John take him to the funeral home."

"That's a homecoming I'm glad I missed," his father said.

They slowly walked into the house. His homecoming had been tarnished but not ruined by Ben's lynching.

"Come on into the house, son. I've got your favorite breakfast on the table," his mother interjected.

When Oceans saw the table layout, he thought, *I'll be damned. She did know.*

It was like old times—crisp bacon, ham, sausage, grits, eggs, smothered potatoes, biscuits filled with fresh-churned butter, and homemade jelly. His mother and father just stood by and silently watched him and let him eat his full. When his plate was empty, he asked for more bacon, a flapjack, and another egg, syrup, a tall glass of milk, and black coffee.

"You're going to bust wide open," his mother joked.

Oceans walked out of the house, rubbing his stomach. He had eaten like it was his last meal, and now he was about to bust.

"Come on, son. Let's sit over here and reminisce. We've got a lot of catching up to do."

"Ok, Pop."

"You want a cold glass of lemonade?" his mother, Hester, yelled from inside the house.

"You're reading my mind, Mubba. but I just don't have any room left. I couldn't put one more thing in my stomach."

"Give the boy a chance to catch his breath before you start questioning him, Enoch."

"Keep out of this, Hester. This is a man's thing."

"Men! You think you know everything."

"How's things going at the high school, Pop? You are still there, aren't you?"

"Where else am I going?"

"I don't know how you do it, Pop—working a full-time job and taking care of this place."

"You do what you got to do, son."

"I see the Klan ain't slowed down, still killing at will."

"They were good for a while, but now that the war is over and the young men are coming home again, they're getting bad again, in fact, worse than before. The KKK lynched a man over in Bower County last week and terrorized another family not far from here just the other day and now Ben. People are leaving now faster than they ever have. It's that black migration thing. That Chicago paper called the *Defender* has been encouraging families to migrate north. Now, there's a rumor that the city is short of farm labor, and they're trying to stop colored folks from leaving. Ain't that something? They treat us like shit, but they don't want us to leave."

"Watch your language in front of your son, Enoch."

"Hell, Hester, I'm sure he's heard worse in the army."

"That doesn't mean he has to hear it from you."

"According to the papers, anyone caught with a *Defender* newspaper will be jailed. They banned the paper from the whole state of Mississippi, they say."

"Can they do that, Pop?"

"Well, they doing it, ain't they? We still get it though. Just have to sneak it in and pass it around."

"You know, Pop, I thought race relations would get better after the war, but it's gotten worse. White GIs were discriminating against black GIs even in London, and American officials backed them up. Seems like we fought for nothing. Our lives are exactly the same."

"I think it may be worse, son. By the way, how come you're just getting home? The war's been over almost eight months. We're gonna be into June pretty soon."

"After I got all of my back pay and mustered out, I spent some time in France, London, and I stopped in New York and spent some time with a soldier that I met in London."

"Why didn't you write?" his mother asked, walking up to them. "You knew we were worried."

"I know I should have, Mubby, but somehow I never got around to it."

"You know how kids are, Hester. They don't think. I see you got yourself a new car."

"It's not new, Pop. I bought it in New York. It's a 1939 Chevy."

"Makes my old truck look like a World War 1 relic. And my boy is a sergeant. You must have done something right in the war."

"Anything I can help you do, Pop?"

"There's always something to do around here, son. You just relax and we'll talk about that tomorrow."

"Have you seen Kenny or Leon lately?"

"Yeah, son. They're both back. They came by to see us and find out if you were back. I heard they were hanging out down at Red's Juke Joint."

"Is that place still open?"

"It's the only place colored folks can go to dance, listen to live music, enjoy some blues, and hear the latest gossip other than the VFW club, and that's not open every day. Oh, yeah, there's always a *Chicago Defender* or two being passed around at both places in spite of the ban."

"I picked up a *Defender* at church last Sunday if you want to see it!" his mother yelled from the kitchen.

"Do you ever see Asantehemaa and Yeboa at church?"

"Not every Sunday, but they do come every once in a while. Since Obiri was lynched, they haven't been as active."

"Does Yeboa still have the shop open? After I get settled, I'm thinking about working with him. It's a good business, and I think we can make a good living, and I think Obiri would like it too."

"So. Tell me, son, what happened to you over there in the war? Why did they think you were missing and probably dead?"

"It's a long story, Pop. I was captured and put in a German prison camp."

"Now that's something. You went all the way to Europe to go to prison."

"You know what, Pop? It was just like you told me a long time ago. The army is segregated, and most of the leaders are prejudiced against colored soldiers. Even in boot camp, we were separated. We got the same training the whites got, but not as much. We were too busy doing kitchen duty or digging latrines and any other menial jobs they could find. Even with that, some of us did well in combat training and marksmanship. I was among the few, white or colored, who qualified as an expert in marksmanship, the best there is, and they made me a truck driver, driving supplies to the white troops on the frontline. Can you imagine that? The white recruits who qualified as experts were sent to sniper school. What does that tell you? I admit, I was disappointed and mad, and I complained. The base commandant told me that colored boys aren't smart enough for sniper school, and I probably just got a lucky shot anyway. When I asked about Officers Candidate School, the captain just looked at me like I was crazy. Later I heard that a Negro named Robinson was in OCS.

"Then after boot camp, they sent me and most of the other colored solders to the motor pool, menial jobs like mess duty or digging latrines. After about a month of driving supplies to the frontline, my truck hit a land mine. I was lucky enough to live through it. That's when I was captured by the Germans and thrown into a concentration camp in northern France. I soon escaped with some French freedom fighters, but the army didn't know any of that. They thought I was dead until I started sending messages to them about German plans. A lot of my new friends were hurt and killed. I was lucky and never even got a scratch. That's about all I can tell you, Pop. I spent the next five years fighting with the French underground. I've got the Knight of the Legion of Honour medal in my bag to prove it."

"That's quite a story, son. How did you make sergeant?"

"That was a freak thing. I saved a white captain's life, and he gave me a battlefield promotion."

"Have you decided what you're going to do now after all that excitement?"

"Right now, Pop, I just want to relax and not think about it." He hated to lie to his father, but he couldn't tell him his real plans.

"How are things going at the high school, Pop?"

"Nothing's changed. They still treat me like I'm colored. Your mother's still complaining about the lack of textbooks and the bad condition of the ones that they have. I still borrow books from the white school when I can. They don't even miss them because they got more than they need, and the black school don't have enough, and the ones they have are hand-me-downs from the white school. Your mother suspects the mayor of stealing money from the colored school budget and giving it to the white school as if they need it. The white school gets new books every two years, and we get their hand-me-downs. Most of them are torn and mutilated. As if that's not enough, she's constantly worried about the Klan showing up one night and burning the school down just out of meanness."

Oceans spent the rest of the day at home just resting and getting reacquainted with the place and visiting with his mother and father.

He walked around the yard, reliving those carefree days when he and his friends played marbles, mumble peg, stickball, and hide-and-seek. That tree that they used to climb didn't seem so tall now as it did then. Their house sat on stones about three feet off the ground, and his friends would crawl under it and listen when he was getting a whipping. There were some good memories from that backyard and a bad one too.

He saw his first lynching from his backyard. He was playing when a terrified black man came running down the street. Men in white sheets and hoods were chasing him and caught him across the street. He was curious, so he continued to watch. His father heard the commotion and ran outside just in time to see the Klan members hanging a man from a tree across the street in their neighbor's yard. Not a pretty sight for a six-year-old to witness.

His father grabbed him and rushed him into the house. By this time, he was screaming hysterically. Not one to hold back anything from his son, his father sat him down and explained. "Son, you're only six years old, but it's time you knew about a ruthless bunch of thugs that call themselves the knights of the Klu Klux Klan, and they prey on colored people. What they did to that man is called lynching. I know that you don't fully understand this now, but as you grow older you will."

"But why?" he asked innocently.

"Because they can," his father answered honestly.

"But what did he do? Was he bad?"

"He was colored like you and me."

"Will they do that to us?"

"If we're not careful."

"When I get big, I'm going to do something to them."

That was a memory he'd like to forget, he thought as he continued his browsing. He was a precocious child, and even at six years old, he understood everything.

Oceans woke up the next morning to the familiar sounds from his childhood. There was a squirrel on his windowsill that he could have sworn was the same one from his school days. He inhaled the aroma of his mother's frying bacon and chicken, which floated up from the kitchen making his mouth water. For a few minutes, he was transformed back to his childhood.

Breakfast was always his favorite meal, so he wasted no time getting to the kitchen. After eating one of his mother's huge breakfasts, he stepped out on the back porch to look for his father whom he knew would be in the garden right after breakfast.

"It's surprising how quickly weeds can sprout up and choke the life out of plants," his father was saying out loud as he hoed and sweated.

"Seems like I just weeded this garden yesterday," he was complaining and trying to keep the sweat from dripping down into his eyes. Seemed like the sun was aiming directly at him.

"Pop! Are you talking to yourself?" Oceans called from the back porch."

"Do you see anyone else out here, son?"

It was his first full day home after five years away. He didn't know what to do with himself. He thought maybe he could help his father with chores around the yard and fields. So he went to his father and said, "What's on the menu for today?"

"Nothing but leisure for you, son. You can make yourself useful in a few days."

"Come on, Pop. I can't just sit around."

"Don't worry, son. There'll be plenty for you to do later."

"Looks like you could use some help in the garden. Look how you're grunting and sweating."

"That's part of the fun, son. Now, go sit down. I got this."

After his father finished and went into the kitchen, he wandered around the house aimlessly for a while, looking at the family pictures on the wall. Outside, he walked under the tall tree that he used to climb when he was a child. It had shrunk to only half its original height. *Wonder how that happened.* He saw the storage shed, which he decided was the perfect place to hide the sniper rifle, night goggles, bullhorn, and field glasses.

"You look lost, son," his father commented coming out on the back porch. "Why don't you run up to Red's bar? You might run into some of your old friends. Who knows?"

"That's a good idea, Pop. I'll see you later. I'm going up to Red's."

RED'S JUKE JOINT

Time may have stood still in the rest of Caloosa, but not at Red's. Red had made some big changes. He now had a mini library in the rear corner of his place, which the city of Callosa didn't even have for Negroes. Looked like over eighty books. Oceans was surprised to see a few men and women reading as they had a drink. He had upgraded the jukebox, put in a little stage for live entertainment, added a piano and drums and bongos. He had modernized the interior and got rid of those hard bar stools for cushion tops, had a whole new bar built, and added new tables and chairs. The place reminded Oceans of the clubs in Harlem on Lenox and Seventh Avenue in New York. Red even had a little kitchen. Now he had food and drink and a show.

As usual, Red had his head in a book. Even though he had been too young to get in Red's Juke Joint when he left for the war, everyone knew about Red's passion for books. He was an avid reader, and many of the less-educated colored people came to him for advice. As kids—and not knowing any better—they had laughed at him because they couldn't understand his obsession with books. He was a lot older than they were and chased them out of his bar a thousand times, but they continued to try to slip inside. Now that he was old enough, it was going to be different.

Muddy Waters was playing on the jukebox when he walked in.

"Still the best blues in town," Oceans commented as he looked around.

Red looked up at him just like he had seen him yesterday and said, "Come on in, Oceans. Good to see ya."

"Hey, O," a familiar voice whooped from a table in the shadows along the wall. "Am I seeing a ghost? Shit, man, I thought you was dead."

"What's happening, Youngblood?" Oceans yelled just as excited. Then he was embarrassed. He had used one of those old childhood nicknames acquired so long ago that he had almost forgotten that his real name was Milton. They had been tight since they were kids.

"Word is that you were missing in action."

Laughing, Oceans called back, "Naw, man, I knew where I was all the time."

"So what happened?"

"It's a long story, chief, and I'm trying to forget it. Anyway, I been back two days. I just been laying low, you know, trying to get back in the groover."

"I know, man. These cotton fields ain't no joke."

"I'm not swinging with cotton, never did. I'm just glad to be back."

"Grab a seat, man. Hey, Red, bring my man a beer. You look different, O, harder, meaner, but you ain't never took no shit off nobody anyway, not even whitey. Have you seen Juvenile since you been home? He's been back about two months."

"I see you're doing it too. His name is Leon, remember?"

"He's still Juvenile to me. He just got out of jail."

"Ain't seen nobody yet."

"So what chew gonna do now, O? Ain't nothing happening here."

"Ain't made no plans yet, just kicking it with my parents."

"Hey, O, over here," a voice sounded from across the room during a lull in the music.

Kenny and Leon were waving over in the corner. "I'll check you later, Blood, I mean Milton. Let me go holler at my boys."

They hadn't seen each other in over five years, and everybody knew it. The celebration was loud, boisterous, and rowdy. Red didn't even try to restrain them. He understood that they were glad to see each other and glad to be alive. He even bought a round of drinks and asked if he could join them, which they quickly agreed too.

"It's good to have you boys back from the war over there."

"I wasn't in the war over there," Leon volunteered, "but I did plenty of fighting."

"I know where you were, Leon. As I was saying, we haven't exactly been at peace here in Caloosa."

"Meaning what, Red?" Oceans asked.

"Meaning the KKK has been up in arms, lynching, burning, and maiming. They been giving us a fit. The Germans and the Japanese couldn't have been much worse. If it was me, I wouldn't have come back. If I ever get away from Mississippi, I'm going to stay away."

"Why don't you just leave, Red?"

"I've got a thriving business here, and I can't leave that."

"Well, we got family here," Kenny answered. "We can't just jump up and leave."

"Believe me, I thought about it," Leon declared.

"Too bad we couldn't find a way to force an unconditional surrender from the Klan like we did Germany and Japan," Oceans remarked.

"Don't forget about Jim Crow. Those laws are more deadly than the KKK," Red reminded them.

"You've been around awhile, Red. Tell us about Jim Crow laws. I know they're against colored people, but I don't know what they are or where they came from," Oceans admitted.

"I've heard my father complaining about Jim Crow this and Jim Crow that, but he never said who he was."

"It's not a who. It's a what," Red went on to explain. "From what I've read, it started with a song and a dance and ended up being a plague for colored people. Back in the 1800s, a white man who called himself Thomas "Daddy" Rice put on some old clothes and some blackface and started imitating a decrepit old black man while singing a minstrel song that he called 'Jump Jim Crow' and dancing. Jim Crow became the name of a popular dance for a while, but it later became the name of some special laws that colored folks had to dance to. These laws stole back our freedom, eliminated our equal rights by promising us separate but equal treatment, and we fell for it because we didn't know the white meaning of *equal*, but it didn't take long for us to find out. The white man's definition of *equal* is inferior treatment, facilities, and education, segregated hotels, theaters, restaurants, transportation, the military, and anything else that might benefit the colored race. Colored rights and full citizenship was ripped right out from under us. We couldn't even vote and, in many states, could be killed or maimed with impunity for even trying. It must have been hard for the white lawmakers to keep a straight face when they wrote 'separate but equal.' Then to make matters worse, the KKK got behind these laws and added fear and terror to reinforce the already-discriminatory nature."

"How do you know all of this, Red?"

"Leon," Red elaborated, "I do something these white folks just don't want colored people to do. I read and I listen. You'd be surprised how many crackers come in here. After a few drinks, they talk about everything. I hear all of their business. They seem to think that because I'm black and own a bar, I'm dumb. I let them keep thinking that. Knowledge can be powerful if used the right way. True. There's some things you can't change, but if you know about them, at least you can try. Take the Klan for instance. For the most part, they're a secret society, and colored folks are not strong enough to tackle the whole organization, and even though we know who some of them (who live among us) are, we can't openly challenge them without endangering our families and other innocent families. The only possibility is to defeat them a few at a time by catching them in the act of violence against a colored victim and stopping them in a way that scares the whole local group. It would have to be done in a way that would not reveal that the person doing it was black."

"You mean like someone else in a hood?" Oceans reasoned.

"Right, but I have no idea how that could be done. Wow, sorry, guys, I have no idea how I got off into that. Look. You guys haven't seen each other in a long time, and you don't need me over here interfering. Welcome home, Oceans."

Oceans had been in and out of trouble part of his young life unknown to his parents. Following Leon, Oceans had gotten into trouble several times as a teenager. One of the times, Oceans had stood lookout while Leon stole the mayor's car just for fun. The idea was to take it to the city dump and dump it. It was supposed to be a funny prank. The car was well known, so they knew they had to dump it fast. When they got to the junkyard, Leon dropped him off at the gate while he dumped the car. There was a sheriff's car patrolling the junkyard when Leon drove in, and he was arrested after taking a beating. Leon ended up spending two months in a work camp. Oceans was with him and should have gone to jail too, but Leon kept his name out of it.

Caloosa only had two city buses, and Negroes had to ride in the back of them. Leon and Oceans came up with the bright idea of breaking into them and loosening all of the front seats. Before they finished the last one, Oceans had to go behind some bushes to pee. While he was peeing, the sheriff rolled up and busted Leon. Someone had seen them and notified the sheriff. When Oceans came around the bushes, the sheriff was cuffing Leon. He started over to give himself up, but Leon motioned him off with his head. He got time in jail for that offense.

Leon's reputation got so bad that Ocean's mother banned him from their house and forbade him from associating with Leon. Neither his mother nor father ever found out about his part in some of the misdeeds that Leon was accused of. Against his mother's wishes, he continued to associate with Leon but drew the line at doing anything dishonest again. To Leon's credit, he tried to keep out of trouble. He still considered him one of his best friends.

"So, Leon, how long were you in jail this time?"

"Four years for robbery. I know you're disappointed in me, Oceans, but I just can't help myself. I see myself getting ready to do something wrong, and the next thing I know, I'm doing it."

"Maybe you've got to much idle time on your hands."

"I can't paint, fix cars, farm, or teach school. I refuse to pick cotton, and I'm tired of sitting around doing nothing, so I steal."

"Listen to yourself, Leon. You're not making sense. You're making excuses. Can't you talk to him, Kenny?"

"What can I tell him, Oceans? I'm in the same shape. I think I'm going back in the navy. It wasn't great, but it was better than here. At least I can see the world."

"Come on. Cheer up. This ain't no funeral. Let's have some fun."

The conversation with Red had stimulated the thoughts that were already in Oceans's mind, and the rescues he had made on the way home had given him the confidence to believe his plan would work. A colored man could have a hidden identity just as easily as a white man. All he needed to do was hide his face and disguise his voice, which he had easily done. Once he put on the black Klan sheet and hood, he was a another person entirely. He could mimic a white man, and who would know the difference? It was dangerous for sure, but it worked.

He thought about the black men he had helped on the highway. It had amounted to the same thing except instead of wearing a sheet, he stood behind a tree in the dark and mimicked a white man. Suddenly, the little doubt about what he had in his mind was gone. He already had the black sheets and the experience. All he had to do was wait for the Klan to strike and then attack. The colored community would never be implicated. White people would be suspicious of each other. All he needed now was a way to find out what the Klan planned to do before they could do it.

He was surprised at how well the Klan paraphernalia turned out, considering that he had never dyed anything before. It looked menacing enough to intimidate the average person. He was about to impact the lives of every Negro in Caloosa who ever feared the Klan.

Seven Days Later . . . Funeral

The little church was standing-room only. The crowd overflowed out the door and into the street.

Ben's funeral was meant to be a short happy celebration of his life, but because of the nature of his death, it became prolonged and sad. There were a lot of sad songs. Friends spoke too long and too passionately. The sermon was long and emotional, driving people to hysterics. His mother became emotional and broke down, but his father managed to stay composed. Oceans declined to speak. He didn't trust himself to maintain his self-control and keep a cool head.

When it was over, they took the long trip to the colored cemetery to say a final goodbye to Ben.

After leaving the cemetery, Oceans followed John Henry to Red's for a final drink and goodbye. John was following the mass migration to the north as the black newspaper, *Defender*, called it. He was fed up with the KKK and the Jim Crow laws. Thousands of colored families were leaving the South searching for a better life.

CHAPTER 6

Steve Grayson

The baby had been crying all night; she was in a lot of pain. Neither Steve Greyson nor his wife, Annie, had gotten a wink of sleep. He was in his truck at first light, driving the five miles to town to get some medicine. His timing was perfect. They were just opening when he and his son walked in. Liniment and turpentine were what he needed and the owner's wife got them and placed it on the counter. But before he could pay for it, a white customer walked into the store and stepped up to the counter in front of him. The clerk promptly took their order, forgetting all about Steve. Then a couple more came in, and he had to wait again. His son, whom he had brought with him because his wife, Annie, was taking care of the baby, was starting to get irritable. He tried to tell the clerk that this was an emergency; his baby was very sick with the colic, but the owner interrupted, called him a nigger, roughly pushed him back, and said, "Wait your turn."

Finally, he couldn't take it anymore. He went berserk and started breaking things, throwing things. "I want my baby's medicine, and I want it now!" he demanded.

"That's it, boy! Get out of my store and stay out!" the owner yelled while pushing Steve toward the door.

But Steve had been pushed too far already and fought back. Blood flew all over him when he punched the owner in the nose, breaking it, and then hit him again. "I want my baby's medicine now, or I'm going to break your damn neck! I may end up being killed, but you won't be here to see it!"

"Give him his medicine and get him out of my store!" the owner whined.

Steve took his medicine and laid his money on the counter. He knew he had messed up already, and he didn't want to add robbery to the incident.

Oceans was meeting Kenny at Red's for lunch and goodbye drinks. He was leaving to go back to the navy on the evening Greyhound bus. They were toasting Kenny's future when Red walked up and sat down. "You're leaving at a good time, Kenny, because we're about to have another lynching tonight."

"What do you mean?"

"You remember Steve Greyson, don't you?"

"Steve Greyson? Yeah, lived down by Harper Lane near the old sawmill. He's a few years older than we are. Yeah, that's him, good-looking guy, fixes cars?"

"What happened? Why would they lynch him?"

"He went berserk over at Riley's general store this morning. He started yelling, cursing, and throwing things, busted up the store pretty good, broke out the front window, and called Riley's wife a white slut bitch, then he beat up Riley when he tried to stop him. Word is he was in the store first thing this morning trying to buy some medicine for his sick baby, and they kept putting white people ahead of him. He told them his baby was sick, and he had to get the medicine home, but they just said, 'Get to the back of the line, nigger.' He just cracked, said he couldn't take it anymore. You can believe the Klan will be paying him a visit tonight as soon as they can get together. Mr. Riley is an active member of the Klan anyway."

"That's a shame," Oceans suddenly said impatiently. "Look Kenny, Leon, I just remembered something. I've got to run. I'll check you later, Leon. Good luck, Kenny."

"Wonder where he's going in such a hurry," Leon mumbled. "He left half his drink, but since we're friends, I'll finish it for him."

My first test in Caloosa, Oceans thought. *We'll see if a man in a black sheet can save Steve Greyson.* While he was getting ready, he noticed some black sheet that was left over and, on impulse, cut out some images of a hood and sheet to take with him and maybe even leave as a calling card. Black Sheet was here.

"But why did you do it, Steve?"

"I just couldn't take it anymore. I had Junior with me, and Ruth was laying here sick. I couldn't let him see me be less than a man. I'm a man, Annie, not just when I'm around colored folks, but around whites too. I'm tired of kids younger than my son calling me boy. I'm tired of being pushed around because God colored me black."

"But you know they gonna be coming for you. They can't let you get away with that. You busted up the store, called Mrs. Riley a bitch and a slut, and busted up Mr. Riley and broke his nose with colored folks and white folks watching. I swear I don't know why they didn't lynch you then. We got to run. You got to get out of here now before they come for you. Lord knows I couldn't stand it."

"I can't run and leave you and the kids. These animals would lynch you and them if they couldn't find me. They won't be here 'til after dark anyway. They feel braver with after dark. Anyway, if I run we go together."

"You mean just leave the house and everything?"

"Not everything. We take our lives and our future with us. There's no future for us here anymore anyway. Even before what I did today, there was no future. Besides Junior was with me. They may kill him anyway and you too. Now come on, woman, grab a few clothes, get our savings, and get in the car. We got to get out of this county. I'm taking my gun. If they catch us, I'm going to fight."

"They won't come until dark. Let's take as much as we can.

Steve Greyson shook his head as he looked around the barn where he had his mechanics shop. He had put a lot of work and money into this shop to make it state of the art, and he hated to leave it. But he knew that he and his family were no longer safe here. The Klan would be coming for him as soon as it was dark. They had already wasted too much time. He wondered if he would ever live in a world where the color of your skin didn't determine your worth. He was leaving a lifetime of work behind him, but he did it once, and he would do it again. Right now he couldn't even imagine what the future would be like. But in spite of all that, he wasn't sorry about what he had done, and he would never give up. He wished he had kicked him a few times too.

Oceans got to Steve's house just after dust dark. He didn't see Steve or his wife, so he found a good place about 150 yards away. It was perfect because he could stand in the shadows and then step out where the full moon would be shining directly on him like a spotlight, making him look surreal. It was a good place to make his first appearance when the Klan arrived. Next, he slipped down and put up a few Black Sheet cutouts then got out of sight and slipped his black sheet and hood on, picked up his sniper rifle and bullhorn, and waited. He didn't have to wait long.

Steve and his family were just coming out the door when two pickup trucks drove down the lane toward his place. There were trees and foliage on each side of the lane. The forest area was full of birds, animals, and insects, yet not a sound came from within. It was as if the whole area was holding its breath, as if the pending violence was palpable. The peaks of the white hoods pointed toward the truck roofs could be seen from the woods as the trucks sped by. There were eyes watching from cover, eyes that belonged to people who wanted to do something but knew they couldn't. They outnumbered the men in the truck but were no match for those that would follow and attack their homes and families if they attacked them. All of Steven's neighbors knew what he had done and what the consequence would be. They didn't believe that this was a lynching offense, but then what wasn't where blacks were concerned?

Steve and his family were all packed and climbing into the truck when the Klan turned into his yard. He had underestimated the time it would take them to come. His wife saw them first and grabbed the children and just said, "Lord, help us."

Steve turned with his gun ready to kill to protect his family, but he was too late. Five Klansmen were on him before he knew it, forcefully dragging him away from his car when Oceans started shooting. In spite of his intentions, Steve hadn't had a chance to use his weapon. He had failed. He should have gotten out sooner. The Klansmen were repeatedly striking him and trying to drag him toward a nearby tree when high-powered rifle shots suddenly started hitting the ground, causing instant panic.

At first no one knew where the shots were coming from or who was firing them. Then a voice rang out.

Oceans had stepped out of the shadows where the full moon would be shining directly on him like a spotlight and the black sheet and hood could be clearly seen, making him look surreal. He hoped it would give them nightmares forever.

"Over here, gentlemen!" Oceans snapped. "This lynching is over. Release Mr. Greyson at once. This is your one and only warning!" Oceans roared through the bullhorn in his most bloodcurdling white voice that reverberated throughout the area, even shocking the people hiding in the woods.

"Who the hell is that clown?" Bill Maloney, one of the Klansmen, wisecracked to the man beside him, "and who is Mr. Greyson?"

Steve's neighbors all over the woods were asking the same question. "Who is that shooting?" Some were slowly creeping to the edge of the woods so they could see. They didn't want to miss anything.

Two more shots rang out, this time killing Jeff Trumps. The Klansmen dived to the ground in panic.

Steve Greyson broke loose and ran to his family.

"Don't shoot!" Riley yelled. "You already killed Jeff Trumps for nothing, for God's sake!"

"Not for God's sake. He came to kill and he died. Do what I tell you, or you will die too."

The people hiding in the woods were spellbound. They wanted to hear everything. Nobody had ever challenged the Klan before.

"Now. Drop your weapons and take off those hoods, and if you hesitate, another one of you will die."

Teeth bared, one of the more militant Klansmen snarled, "I ain't dropping my gun and taking off my hood for nobody, especially a white piece of trash wearing a black sheet and hood."

A shot rang out, and the Klansman fell with a bullet through the head. Panic stricken, one of the Klansmen shrieked, "Hold it! Hold it! He shot Maloney too. Take off your sheets and hoods before he kills us all!"

"Now take all of the money out of your pockets and throw it into the car, and I mean everything. I'm going to send Fred down there to check, and if you still have money, you're going to die."

Steve Greyson and his family just stood there astounded, unable to move, not understanding what was happening. "Now, Mr. Greyson, take your family and leave and good luck."

Steve Greyson just stood there for a second, rooted to the spot. "Go now, Mr. Greyson. What are you waiting for? You're free to go. Don't just stand there in a daze. Get the hell away from here."

As Steve and his family drove away, Oceans shot up the trucks that the Klansmen came in.

"What the hell, he beat up a white man and assaulted a white women and you just let him go. Now you're shooting up our trucks. You're making a big mistake, mister. Who the hell are you? Take off that hood."

"If I do that, I'll have to kill all five of you. Besides, you have more to worry about than Mr. Greyson's whereabouts, Mr. Bonaparte."

"You know my name?"

"I know you well, Andrew, and you, Wesley and Decker. Hell. I sit in the meeting with you every month. Hello, Jim, good to see you again, but I never thought we'd meet like this."

"You sit in a meeting with us. You sound like one of us. Who the hell are you, and why are you doing this?"

"If you don't know, I can't tell you."

Years ago, Obiri had pointed out all of these men to Oceans before he died, and he never forgot their faces. "See those men," he said and called them by name. "They are among the city's top citizens, and they claim to like colored people. But don't believe them. They're all members of the Klan. It's the ones that pretend to like you that you have to watch out for. They're the most dangerous because they have your trust. They're like snakes in the grass—strike without warning."

"How are we supposed to get out of here with no trucks? That's what I want to know."

"Start walking back down the lane the way you came. That's your only choice. And if I were you, I'd walk fast."

Unknown to the would-be lynchers, the whole thing had been witnessed by several blacks hidden in the woods. They later ventured out and took the weapons dropped by the Klan.

While everyone's attention was either on the Klansmen or Steve and his family making their escape, Oceans slipped unobserved into the dark woods and made it to his car, which he had painstakingly hidden behind some foliage. He stored the black sheet and hood and inconspicuously drove back to the main road. He was still a little surprised that it went so well but very pleased with himself.

Steve drove fast and recklessly those first few miles after being rescued from the KKK. His wife constantly looked back through the rear window to see if they were being followed. His son was trembling like a leaf and close to hysteria. Neither could believe their good fortune. "Who was that man who helped us?" Annie asked. "I thought you were dead until he came."

"I don't know. I'd never seen him before. At first, I just stood there confused. I didn't know if he was for us or against us until he said get in the car and go. I know one thing—God is real," Steve mumbled to himself, but his wife heard him and just started praying, thanking God for his blessings and grace.

They passed the Kroger and the Piggly Wiggly store, made it to the main highway, and out of the county going north.

As the terrified Ku Klux Klansmen moved swiftly and cautiously up the pitch-black rural road, unnerving sounds assaulted them from the woods. Grunts, moans, groans, screams, laughs, and other noises were coming from the woods. Rocks, broken limbs, old tires, pipes, broken concrete, and anything else lying around were hurled at them. They knew colored people were lurking behind the trees mocking them in their embarrassment, frustration, and fear. Never had they suffered such a defeat, and to make matters worse, it was by a white man. They were tasting some of their own medicine.

There were a million stars blinking in the sky and even a falling star. Eldon Green wondered if that was an omen of bad things to come. Any other time, they would have been beautiful, but tonight they seemed to be mocking them too. Eldon Green looked back toward Steve Greyson's house and saw a bright light.

"Looks like a barn fire back there. Wonder what that is," he commented.

Andrew Bonaparte didn't even bother to look back. "My guess is that's our vehicles burning."

"Shit," Riley cried out, "I just bought that damn truck. It ain't even paid for yet, and to make matters worse, I had over three hundred dollars in my pocket. I had just left the bank."

"You're worried about your truck and your money after we left Tubbs and Maloney back there on the ground dead. We came out tonight for you. Did you forget?"

Unfazed by the interruption, Riley continued with his rant. "We should come back and burn this whole section down and kill all of these fucking niggers."

"Oh yeah, well, it wasn't the coloreds that killed Tubbs and Maloney. We'll be better off finding that white bastard in the black sheet and killing him."

"What am I going to tell my wife?" Riley continued.

"What are we gonna tell Tubbs's and Mahoney's wives?" Bonaparte countered.

By the time they reached the gas station on the main road where they could call for help, it was past midnight, and the station was closed. They had to break in to use the telephone.

"Who should we call?" Eldon asked.

"Call the sheriff," somebody suggested.

"Are you crazy? We don't want the sheriff to see us like this."

"Call my wife. She'll come get us."

"We may still be able to catch those niggers that got away if we hurry," Riley remarked.

"Riley!" Eldon growled. "You go to hell. And we're calling the sheriff, not your damn wife. This never would have happened if you had just given that nigger the medicine for his damn child."

Aftermath: Oceans after the First Black Sheet Attack

Oceans was exhausted but elated by the time he reached home and stored his disguise. He slowly walked to his room, stretched, and fell onto his bed too tired to take off his clothes.

Sleep came slowly. His nerves were taut, raw, and on edge. He tossed and turned for what seemed like hours, finally getting up and looking out the window into the black night and listening to the insects singing their familiar song. He tried identifying the sounds of the nocturnal insects. The clicking and popping of the bats trying to navigate through the night, the chirping of the crickets, the rhythm of the tree frogs, the vibrations of the cicada, and the lullabies of grasshoppers all were familiar. But the night sounds that he remembered from his childhood didn't comfort him at all. He was more agitated here in Mississippi in KKK territory than he had ever been in German territory. He couldn't relax standing up and couldn't sleep lying down. Still somehow, he made it through the night, finally drifting off to sleep around dawn.

His mother woke him up after what seemed like minutes after he had fallen asleep, but he had slept longer than he thought, and it was almost eleven o'clock.

"Wake up. Wake up. Wake up," she chanted cheerfully. "It's a new day."

Sitting up in bed and wiping the sleep out of his eyes with the back of his hand, Oceans grumbled, "What are you so happy about this morning?"

"You're missing all of the excitement. The party line is about to explode."

"What excitement?"

"Some white guy dressed in a black sheet and hood shot up the KKK and kept them from lynching Steve Greyson. Now everybody is talking about it. You can't even make a phone call, but who wants to when there's so much to listen to on the line. You should hear it. This Black Sheet killed that nasty, hateful scoundrel Jeff Trumps and Bill Maloney. Nobody ever challenged the Klan before. I'm glad Steve got away. I heard what he did, and I was afraid for him. Are you listening to me, Oceans? You're just like your father. Go on. Go back to sleep."

TALK OF THE TOWN

Marge McCoy waited impatiently, pacing the floor in the back of the little country store where she and her family lived. She was anxious for Riley to get home and tell her how he and the others had terrorized that uppity nigger Greyson before finally killing him. She hoped they had made him suffer. The nerve of that nigger sassing her and attacking her husband. She should have told them to get his family too. This would be a fine lesson for her other colored patrons, that they had better stay in their place.

It was getting late, and Riley should have been back by now. *They must really be enjoying themselves killing that nigger,* she thought, *too bad I can't be there to see it.*

Home at last! What had started out to be a routine maiming and lynching had turned into an unexpected nightmare. Who was the guy in the black sheet and where did he come from? Why would another white man interfere with Klan business? How could he face his wife and tell her that not only did Steve Greyson get away, but they also lost their truck too and their expense money?

"Riley! You're finally home. What the hell took you so long? I was about to go crazy. Did you get that uppity-ass nigger? I hope you made him beg. I want to hear all of the details."

"W . . . We grabbed him, bu . . . but there was a little problem."

"What kind of problem? Don't tell me that nigger got away."

"Will you just shut up and let me tell you what happened?"

"Don't holler at me."

"This guy in the black sheet and hood showed up before we could lynch him."

When he told her what happened, she just started screaming and screaming in frustration. "What are we going to do now? That truck wasn't even paid for, and we needed the money to replenish the store. Are you lying to me, Riley? That story about a white man in a black sheet is pretty wild."

The news traveled across the city like a wildfire with a hundred-mile-an-hour wind pushing it. A white man in a black sheet and hood rescued a colored man from the KKK. Every time it was told, it got worse, and the Klan looked worse. An all-out bulletin had been sent out, and the police were out in force looking for him. Only it was a waste of time because they didn't know who to look for—he could have been anybody. Newspaper headlines were screaming for his head. The mayor called a council meeting to discuss this unimaginable, unacceptable, unprecedented, and unbelievable occurrence.

The KKK was out in force in full regalia, blundering around intimidating but powerless. They didn't know where to look or who to look for. They couldn't burn crosses in the white neighborhood to coerce whites into informing on the culprit even if they knew his identity. They looked and felt like fools.

The police department flooded the woods around Steve Greyson's place with police officers, private citizens, and dogs looking for clues and questioning his neighbors who said they didn't see or hear anything. Besides, Steve was long gone.

"How can you not know something," the sheriff roared, "when everybody's talking about it? Shots were fired. Five men were assaulted, two killed, and two trucks were burned, five rifles were stolen, and you want me to believe that nobody saw or heard anything? Do I look stupid to you?"

A nearby farmer cleared his throat at that remark.

"You got something to say?" the sheriff retorted.

"Huh, you forgot to mention that a colored man was almost lynched."

"Don't get smart with me, nigger."

"Just trying to help, sur."

It had been many years since the little town of Caloosa had had this much excitement. Everyone wondered who this mysterious white man in the black sheet was, where he came from, and why he helped a colored man. Who were the other men with him?

The field workers cheered him on the flatbed truck driving them to the cotton fields. Maids and housekeepers quietly applauded him at work. Sharecroppers talked about it in the fields. Bar flies toasted him in the bars. The man some called Black Sheet was a hero in the black neighborhood.

There was something even bigger and more important than Black Sheet happening in the colored community. A mass exodus was taking place all over the South.

The appearance of Black Sheet had no effect on this mass movement that was taking place in Caloosa and all over the South. The colored population was migrating north, east, and west, and this collective movement was affecting the economy of the South. The workforce that had been taken for granted by the white population was moving away, and steps had to be taken to stop them.

THE GREAT ESCAPE
Migration

Ten-year-old Bobby and Robbie were walking barefoot down the gravel road, a pocket full of marbles in each of the pockets of their baggy pants. Calloused feet didn't even notice the different-sized rocks that assaulted them. Their minds were on the game of marbles that they planned to win before they went north. All the best shooters in Caloosa would be there, including the so-called champ. Bobby planned to change that, but so did his brother, Robbie. They were leaving for Chicago in two days with their mother and intended to take the championship with them. They couldn't even tell their friends they were moving. Something about migration chasers trying to stop them and bring them back. They didn't even know what a migration was.

When they got to the game, they both pulled out their best shooters.

"Well, look who's here. It's the twins bringing us some more marbles. How many marbles did you bring us, boys?"

"As many as you can take, chump," ten-year-old Bobby answered with a smirk on his face.

"I was going to take it easy on you, Bobby, or is it Robbie? But since you're trying to be funny, I'm gonna take all of your marbles and wipe you out."

"You got to bring some to get some."

It was friendly but serious. "Sorry, fellows, but we're taking, not giving. This is for keeps."

They drew ten-foot circles, and each player had to put in seven marbles that were lined up in the shape of an X. There were fifteen circles with two players to a circle. This was some serious stuff. Both Bobby and Robbie won the lag to be first shooter at their circle, and they didn't waste a shot. The ducks were flying out of the ring like they had wings. Only instead of flying south, they would be taking the train north. Every time they knuckled down to shoot, they hit one of the ducks lined up in the ring. They won game after game as the losers stood around sulking. Some even tried to cheat.

"That don't count," Bobby challenged when Russell knocked one out the ring.

"What do you mean it don't count? You saw me knuckle down and knock that pink marble out of the ring fair and square."

"I saw you hunch over the line, and that's cheating."

"I saw it too," another player said. "You were fudging. Put it back."

"See that bumblebee with the yellow and black stripe right in the middle?" Robbie called in another ring. "That's a dead duck!"

He hit the bumblebee, knocked it out, and stayed in the ring. Now he really got busy and knocked the rest of the ducks out, ending the game.

In his next game, the current champ was Robbie's opponent and knocked four ducks out and looked like he would empty the ring, then his shooter glanced off a duck, and it didn't go out, but his shooter stayed in the ring. Based on the agreement before the game, his shooter became a legitimate target. Robbie knocked the shooter out and got the shooter and the four marbles the shooter had won.

Robbie, as usual, rubbed it in, and the fourteen-year-old ex-champ was a bad loser especially to a ten-year-old boy. Robbie and Bobby played each other for the championship, and Bobby lost, and that ended the games.

"I won so many marbles, I can hardly hold my pants up," Robbie bragged on the way home.

"You almost won a black eye too talking your stuff. You know Rease got a quick temper."

"Yeah. I thought for sho' he was gonna swing on me."

Walking home, they saw a group of deputies chasing some colored families with bags away from the train station. They knew what that was all about.

Bobby, being inquisitive, wanted to know what the colored migration was all about. When they got home, their mother and aunts were discussing the migration, and they quietly sat down to listen.

"We're free, but they still treat us like slaves," their mother pointed out emotionally. "We're damned if we stay and damned if we try to go. What do they want from us?"

"That easy," her sister Clara answered. "If they let us go, they have to work their own sharecrops, take care of their own houses, raise their own children, pick their own cotton, do their own cooking, and wipe their own asses."

"Easy, girl, the kids are listening."

"Oh, you're home," their mother acknowledged. "I know you been wondering why we're leaving your grandmother and your friends and moving north to Chicago. Well, the main reason is to have a better life, a life without the Jim Crow system. We're going to live in a place called Bronzeville. I'll be able to get a better job, go to nursing school, or even take business classes and learn how to type so I can work in an office typing instead of the fields picking cotton or cleaning somebody's house. At least I can do better for me and my family than I'm doing here. You'll have a better life too, more freedom to go to school, to the movie, to stores like Woolworths, to ride the bus and sit wherever we want to, even to walk down the sidewalk and not have to step off for some white man or woman."

"You mean we wouldn't have to sit in the back?"

"No, son, we could sit anywhere."

"Even next to white people, Momma?"

"Even next to white people, son. It's not just us. Thousands of colored people are moving north to find a better life. The newspaper calls it a colored migration.

"You ever see the flocks of birds flying south just before winter. Well, we're like them, only we're going north to stay. They migrate south because the warm weather is better for them and their families. We migrate north because the opportunities are better for us and our families. But we have to leave something we love behind. Every family that goes north has to sacrifice something. They leave their homes, most of their belongings, and the only life they've ever known. We all start off even when we get north. We start with nothing, and some of us know nobody. At least we're better off than our ancestors 100 years ago. They had to walk, and if they got caught, they were beaten, maimed, or even killed. Maybe Black Sheet's presence will make things better for those who stay.

"Kids, we don't know what we're running to, but we know what we're running from".

STEVE GREYSON'S REACTION

Still not believing their good fortune or really comprehending what had just happened, the Greysons raced down the highway headed north. They just wanted to get out of Mississippi as quick as possible.

Steve Greyson was still trembling from the close call they had just had. He expected to be dead by now. His swollen eyes were fixed on the road ahead. His busted and bloated nose was still inflamed, but the bleeding had stopped.

The night was pitch-black but for what seemed like a million stars in the sky and a bright tunnel ahead of them made by their headlights. They had the highway all to themselves, and that they saw as a blessing. He figured they were in Tennessee now, and some of the small towns that he drove cautiously through were dangerous. He was glad it was dark, and nobody could tell they were black. The fewer travelers they met, the safer they felt they would be. The kids had stopped crying and drifted off to sleep, but not before they asked why the white men wanted to hurt them.

Finally, his wife, Annie, asked the question that had plagued both of their minds. "Who was that white man in the black sheet and hood, and why would he help us? How did he know what happened at the Tracy's?"

It was a question that would go unanswered. There was one thing they both knew. They were grateful. They were blessed, and they were glad to get out of Caloosa, Mississippi, alive.

"What we gonna do, Steve?"

"Where we gonna live."

"Where you gonna work?"

"I'm still a mechanic, Annie."

"Where are we gonna go? We had to leave everything we worked so hard for."

"We're lucky to have that problem, Annie."

"How's that Steve?"

"Think about our other choice."

"Oh!"

They didn't know where or what was ahead, but they knew what was behind, and that's all of the courage they needed. As she talked, his wife, Annie, absentmindedly picked through the stuff that had been thrown into the car by the KKK and suddenly screamed.

Steve panicked and jammed down on the accelerator, speeding up, thinking that the KKK was chasing them. "How close are they?" he asked his wife.

"No! No!" she cried. "Money. Steve, there's over four hundred dollars here. Somebody must have just gone to the bank cause nobody carries this much money around."

"Four hundred dollars! You mean the Klan threw over four hundred dollars in our car?" he said, stuttering and almost losing control of the car.

"I counted it twice," Annie declared.

"Well, count it again."

"It's over four hundred dollars," she stressed. "I can count."

"That's more money than we've ever seen at once. I didn't know how we were going to get started again," Steve admitted.

"I was worried too," Annie conceded.

PREACHER'S STORY

Church started as usual with hymns, an associate minister rousing the congregation, a few prayers, and a touching solo followed by an A&B selection from the full choir and a prayer. Then the pastor walked in and stepped to the pulpit to deliver his sermon.

"Today," he said, "I'm not going to preach. Instead, I'm going to tell you a story. A very true hard-to-believe story about a colored man captured by members of the KKK while innocently walking home from work after midnight and forced to face his own Calvary. Instead of a mountain, they took him into the woods, stripped him of his clothing, beat him with belts, and wrapped him in barbed wire then started to castrate him. Unlike Jesus, this man begged for his life and his manhood, but to no avail. When he realized that death was imminent, he gave up the struggle. Like Shadrach, Meshach, and Abednego, he was facing his own Nebuchadnezzar, and he was trapped in his own furnace facing death.

"Suddenly out of the night, shots rang out, and Klan members began to fall. Those not shot ran, and a white voice in the night commanded one of the wounded Klansmen to remove the wire from the black man and let him go. It was a miracle that only God could perform. When that colored man was freed and turned to thank the white man who freed him by the grace of God, he looked into the face of another colored man. Yes, that's right! He was freed by a black man who was able to disguise his voice, hide behind a tree in the dark, and sound white. Somebody say amen. Hard to believe," he said as he was pulling off his suit coat and then his shirt.

People were wondering what he was up to. When he removed his shirt pandemonium, broke out in the church.

"Look at my body."

The piano was blaring, people were crying. Some were shouting, and very few could stay in their pews.

"I have the barbed wire scars to prove it, "he said, his voice cracking. "I'm that black man. Today I give thanks to a merciful God and a colored man who overcame his own fears to help me. Thank you, Lord. Thank ya."

EMERGENCY MEETING AT CITY HALL

All protocol was forgotten at the city hall meeting following the attack on the KKK and subsequent killing of Jeff Trumps and the rescue of Steve Grayson by a white man dressed in a black sheet and hood. It took a lot of yelling and banging on his desk by the mayor to finally bring the meeting to order.

"Looks like we've got a troublemaker in town, and we're not going to solve the problem by all talking at once. Let's start by hearing the real story from someone who was there.

"So what happened out there, Riley?" the mayor probed.

"Jeff Trumps, one of our most loyal followers, was shot dead by this, uhm, Black Sheet. When you needed to teach a nigger a lesson, he was always the first to volunteer. He was one of our most enthusiastic and devoted nigger haters. Now he's dead long before his time. He'll be missed. Meanwhile that nigger Steve Greyson is laughing all the way north."

"Now let's see if I understand. This nigger came into your store, insulted you, insulted your wife, then beat the living hell out of you, and now he's free as a bird. How did that happen?"

"A man in a black sheet and hood helped him."

The legislative assembly—most of whom were closet members of the KKK—went berserk when they heard that. The city council chambers were in an uproar. Everyone was talking at once. The mayor was trying to restore order, but it was almost impossible.

"Who in the hell is this Black Sheet character you're talking about?" someone was asking angrily. "Where did he come from? How could he interfere? Who was with him? What does he look like?"

"If we knew all of that, we wouldn't be here," the mayor argued. "Evidently all we know is he was wearing black. He shot Jeff, shot up your trucks, made you give all your money to that Greyson nigger, and threatened to kill all of you, then he told Steve Greyson to run all while you all stood there trembling."

"What would you have done, mayor? He had a black hood over his face. He had a high-powered rifle pointed at us, and he had an accomplice that we couldn't see. All we know is that he was white."

"How do you know he's white?"

"I can hear, and he sure wasn't colored. Ask Eldon Green, Andrew Bonaparte, and Braxton—they were there."

"He's right," Eldon verified. "The man in the black sheet was white. Tell you something else funny—he called me by name. It's somebody we know."

"What's his motivation? How do we stop him?"

"That's what we're here to find out, but we can't do it with everyone talking at once. Brax, you were there. Why don't you tell us what happened."

"It was like a nightmare. The rifle he was pointing at us looked like a cannon. I thought for sure we were going to die."

"Oh hell, Braxton, don't be so damn dramatic. Just tell the story," demanded the sheriff.

As Braxton told his story, there were numerous outbursts and alarmed facial expressions. "You mean he was ready to kill?" a council member asked incredulously."

"He did kill. Haven't you been listening?" Riley asked.

"Are you sure you're not exaggerating this just a little?" another member asked.

"Exaggerating my ass," Braxton answered, losing patience. "Two men are dead. Two trucks are destroyed. We had to walk ten miles through a colored neighborhood at midnight. Do you think we'd come in here and make up a story like this? Elden Green and Andrew Bonaparte were there. He called them by name too. They can corroborate my story."

"No need for that, Brax. After all, you're not on trial here."

"Well, it sounds like it."

"It's just that, well, a white man taking the nigger's side is hard to swallow."

"Well, take a look at this," Braxton said, pulling something out of his pocket and holding it up. "I went back by there this morning and found this. He left his calling card. It's a little black cutout of a Klan robe and hood. See if you can choke this down."

On seeing that, bedlam broke out in the chambers again. After the meeting finally calmed down, the chief of police stood up and told everyone to keep their eyes and ears open. "If this is somebody we know, look for suspicious behavior from any of your neighbors and report it. We've got to catch this guy."

After that, the meeting was adjourned with nothing accomplished.

ASANTEHEMAA AND YEBOA

Asantehemaa Afua, Obiri's widow, saw Oceans when he turned on to the lane leading to her house. She called to her son, Yeboa, who was working in the shop Owusu Ansa to see if he could identify the car.

"Maybe it's a new customer," he guessed. "I've never seen it before."

The car pulled up and stopped, and Oceans whom they never expected to see again opened the door.

"You're not a ghost because I don't believe in ghosts and ghost don't drive cars," Asantehemaa proclaimed through a big smile as she welcomed Oceans.

"My brother, you're not dead," Yeboa joked as he ran to embrace his friend. "When did you get home? Where've you been? We missed you."

"Slow down, Yeboa." His mother laughed.

"Sorry, Mother. I'm just glad to see him alive."

"Where's my best girl?"

"Owusu is happily married and living in Elmina, Ghana—a coastal town in West Africa," Asantehemaa declared proudly. "Her father would be so pleased with her."

"Africa? How did that happen?"

"She met an African boy when she went away to Lane College in Tennessee, and after they got married, they said they wanted to go back home. Not many of us think of Africa as home," Ashtehemaa asserted proudly. "And to tell the truth, I'd like to go too, and I will someday."

"How about you, Yeboa? Is that your wish too?" Oceans asked.

"Not me. I'm gonna work in Dad's shop. I get a little work already. Together we could get more if we had the right equipment. I still remember everything Dad taught me. How about you, Oceans?"

"You know he always wanted us to work it together. I think I'd like that, Yeboa."

"Well, come on back to the shop and let me show you what I've been doing."

Oceans parked next to the house then followed Yeboa around to the shop.

"What do you think we need to make this work?" Oceans asked, looking around.

"We've got most of the basic tools—drills, bits, precision micrometers, jigsaws, and stuff. We could start off with small jobs and add on as we go."

"We can't do too much without a lathe, a drill press, and a large workbench grinding wheel. That small one is okay for little jobs, but nothing big," Oceans observed.

"That's a lot of money, Oceans. We can't afford that yet, but we'll get there."

"I've still got my mustering-out money from the army, and this is a good investment for our future. You start checking and see what it's gonna cost. Maybe you can find a used craftsman lathe, but if you can't, check with Sears Robuck and Company and price a new one. On second thought, price all new ones. We don't need any breakdowns. Oh, and price one of those Powermatic table saws too."

"Are you sure, Oceans?"

"As sure as I'm standing here. This is one of my dreams."

Yeboa and the shop were heavy on Oceans's mind as he turned out of the lane, leaving their house. He hoped this career move wouldn't interfere with his main dream to curb the actions of the KKK.

CHAPTER 7

Oceans Looks Around

Now that he had started this Black Sheet thing, Oceans decided that he had better drive around and get reacquainted with the town that he grew up in. He wanted to see any changes that had been made, like dead ends or new streets and houses that could cause confusion to Black Sheet if he was being chased by the Klan.

He was immediately surprised at some of the changes that he saw. Areas that had been overgrown with trees, bushes, weeds, wild flowers were now filled and contained houses and business, and what used to be dead ends were now through streets. Some of the through streets were now dead ends. It was confusing. The area had changed much that he barely recognized it and wouldn't have in the dark. As Oceans, it didn't matter. However, as Black Sheet, it could be the difference between life and death.

Farther down, he saw an airfield of sorts with a crop duster preparing to take off. Continuing on, he saw the new white school building, which brought to mind the black schoolhouse that was actually a converted warehouse. The big surprise of the day was a beautiful little building sitting on a manicured lawn with evergreens and flowers bordering it. This was the new Knights of the Ku Klux Klan headquarters. Just looking at it and knowing what it represented and imagining the deadly plans against blacks that had been hatched in this building gave him a sick feeling and reinforced his determination to rid Caloosa of this malignant tumor that continued to fester and grow.

BIG MOMMA AND RUBY

After discovering this apparent KKK expansion, he lost his taste for driving around and instead decided to stop for a cold Dr. Pepper at Big Momma's little roadside café.

Big Momma was busy shucking green beans and cleaning collard greens and didn't notice him come in. Oceans walked up behind her and kissed her on the cheek, and she jumped, almost spilling the beans sitting in a big bowl in her lap.

"Heavens, boy!" she screamed, looking up at him, doing a double take, and screaming again. "This can't be you! You're dead, killed in the war. My God, boy, you scared me out of my wits. Is that you, Oceans?" she said, looking over the top of her glasses.

"It's me, Big Momma."

"Heck, boy, don't you know Big Momma got a weak heart? Should have known better than to believe you were dead. You too smart to let yourself get killed. What you come back here for? If you get away, stay away—that's what I say. People are running north, and you coming back south."

"Couldn't stay away. I missed your big smile too much."

"You haven't changed. Still full of jive, but Big Momma likes it."

"Hey, Oceans," a voice said from behind him, and he looked back into the prettiest face he had ever seen.

"Hey, uh . . ." He didn't know her name, and he was lost for words.

She saw the frown on his face and said, "You don't know me, do you?" Before he could answer, she continued, "My name is Ruby Asberry. I'm Reverend Asberry's youngest daughter. You once saved me from being raped."

"That . . . that was you?" he stammered.

"Well, I admit, I may have changed a little since then."

"A li-little!" he teased, openly admiring her, and they both started laughing uncontrollably. "Can I buy you a Dr. Pepper and a sandwich, soup, pie, cake?"

"Stop, stop, stop. You can buy me a Nehi orange."

"You kids sit over at that table and get to know each other. I'll bring your drinks."

"Thanks, Big Momma."

Oceans was hypnotized and trying not to show it. He was helplessly drawn to her. It was like they had been best of friends for years as they sat there laughing and talking.

"Why did I never run into you again before I left?"

"You did, and I tried to get your attention several times, but you ignored me. I guess I hadn't changed enough yet—seems the girls that had your attention were a lot hipper than I was at the time."

"Well, I don't know about that, but I do know—and I hope you don't take this wrong—you've more than made up for any shortcomings you may have had then, and believe me, you've got my attention now."

"Why, Oceans, you're making me blush, and that ain't easy."

"And you're making me want to kick myself for missing all those other opportunities to get to know you."

"If that's a line, Oceans, you've got it down pat. I'd better watch myself."

"It may sound like a line, but if you give me the time, I'll prove to you that I'm sincere."

"How much time do you think you're gonna need?"

"Maybe a lifetime. You never know."

They had a good visit and made a date to go out and really get to know each other. Oceans left Big Mommy's completely infatuated.

Other more subtle changes were taking place in white neighborhoods all over Caloosa. Black Sheet had now been twice referred to attending meetings. Thinking Black Sheet was white, thinking Black Sheet was attending meetings, and thinking he must be an acquaintance, people were starting to look at their neighbors with suspicion. Now there was a big reward out on Black Sheet, and white people were becoming even more distrustful of each other.

SUSPICION

Virginia Nash was looking out her back window at her white neighbors a few doors down and thinking about the Black Sheet character that everyone was talking about, and it occurred to her that they had been acting kind of strange lately. Also, they were the only whites in the neighborhood who never attended any of the neighborhood meetings concerning the colored problem. In fact, she had never heard them say anything negative about the blacks.

The man was away from home a lot and came in late the night of the Steve Greyson incident. He could be that Black Sheet fellow. She called the sheriff and reported her suspicions.

That same night, she stood in her window and watched the sheriff and his deputies raid her neighbor, rough him up, and tear his house apart looking for the black sheet and hood, which they didn't find.

Meanwhile all over the white neighborhoods' people were looking at each other skeptically.

BUDDY FROM BOOT CAMP

While passing by the Greyhound station, Oceans saw a passenger step off the bus wearing army fatigues and recognized him from the war. He was changing buses in Caloosa and had about two hours of layover. Oceans went over and invited him to Red's for a drink. After they talked a while, his friend made a confession.

"I did something real dumb," his friend, Jerome, was saying.

"Come on, we all do dumb shit sometimes," Oceans answered.

"Yeah, but not like this."

"So what did you do that was so dumb, shoot yourself in the foot and then find out that the war was over?"

"I brought some live grenades home."

"You brought home live grenades?"

"I said it was dumb."

"What did you do with them? Where are they now?"

"In my bag on the bus, and I hold my breath every time we hit a bump."

"Jerome, you're telling me you got a live grenades on that Greyhound bus."

"Four!"

"Damn, man. You got four grenades."

"Well, I said it was dumb."

"But how? Why?"

"My last day on the base, they had all the colored boys on a working party unloading ammo. A box of grenades broke, and I took four. I guess I was just mad because they made me work on my last day while the white boys who was getting discharged was allowed to just lounge around. I guess I had it in my mind to blow up something. I don't know what. Now, I don't know what to do with them. I can't just throw them away. Somebody may find them and blow themselves up."

An idea occurred to Oceans. "Look, fool, you lucky you didn't blow that bus up. Tell you what. I'll get rid of them for you. I think I know just the place. Get 'em and leave them with me."

"You ain't jiving me, are you?"

"Just get the damn things before I change my mind. You owe me, man."

BLACK WOMAN DON'T TEACH MY CHILD

Little eleven-year-old Nancy Corbett had problems with her math homework every day. Her mother would try to help her and then get frustrated and start fussing and complaining, "Why didn't you listen when the teacher showed the class how to do it?"

One day the maid and housekeeper saw her struggling and asked if she needed help. "I have to ask my teacher tomorrow because my mother tried, but she couldn't do it."

"Let's see it. Oh. This is easy. You just move this number here and subtract this number, and this is the answer."

Nancy was confused, and it showed on her face. It was clear that she didn't understand; this colored woman was supposed to be dumb, yet she did the problem, and her mother couldn't do it.

Two days later, she had a problem with her reading and her math, and again her mother couldn't figure it out, so she said, "That's okay. I'll ask Betsy."

"Betsy!" her mother snapped. She followed her daughter to where her housekeeper was washing the windows and listened while Betsy solved both problems and never stopped washing the windows.

"It's okay, Momma," Nancy boasted. "I knew Betsy could do it easy."

That evening, Nancy's mother told Betsy, "We won't need your services after today."

"But why, Mrs. Corbett? I thought you were pleased with my work, and Mr. Corbett said he was pleased with my cooking. Have I done something wrong?"

"I don't need no smart-ass nigger working for me. Now get out of my house and don't come back!"

CROP DUSTER

"How often do those crop dusters taking off from Sunny Pike Field and fly over the city to dust crops on the other side of town?" Oceans asked his father.

"Crop dusters? Every Tuesday and Thursday. Why?"

"Just wondering."

Oceans spent two days making a banner ten feet long with big block letters that could be seen from a mile away.

Seemed like a million stars lit up the sky over the field where the crop duster was parked, and they provided just enough light to save Oceans from lighting a lantern. He was very nervous as he walked across the grass, approaching the plane. For one thing, he was afraid there may be snakes around, and he was thinking about some of the farfetched stories he had heard about a coach whipper snake that would run up your pants' leg. Naturally, he didn't believe all of that stuff, but it was still on his mind.

He had the banner he had made rolled up into a ball so that when the plane took off, it would unfurl and display his message. It only took a short time to attach the banner to the tail of the plane and get back to his car. He knew crop dusters sometimes pulled banners. So he doubted the pilot would think much of the banner rolled up behind his plane. Now all he could do was wait for the plane to take off in the morning and hope it turned out all right.

The crop duster pilot saw the banner folded up and attached to his plane when he arrived for work. It wasn't the first time he had found a banner attached to the plane, so he thought nothing of it. He was never told in advance when he would be pulling a banner, so he took off without giving it a second thought.

Oceans got up early that Thursday morning and found a good spot to look for the plane.

He smiled when he saw the banner unfurl displaying his message— BLACK SHEET VENGEANCE, KKK DOWNFALL.

The message showed up perfectly as the plane flew over. Then Black Sheet leaflets started raining down into Caloosa streets and yards.

"I wonder how the Klan likes that," Oceans asked and answered himself, "Not a bit."

The crop duster flying over Caloosa twice a week was a common sight, and normally caused little or no notice. But today people were looking up and pointing up. There was excitement, confusion, approval, and open contempt for the message. There were people for and some against the Klan. To no one's surprise, the reactions were broken down along racial lines.

Most of the residents of Caloosa didn't have private telephone service; therefore, they were on party lines. There was no privacy on party line service because anyone who picked up the phone could listen in, and many listened in on a regular basis and knew everybody's business. The party lines were jumping. The excitement was alive with trepidation and apprehension. People were calling the mayor. Klansmen were calling each other. The city police and the sheriff's office were bombarded with angry calls. Citizens were screaming for them to do something. The phone at the Dixie Air Service office that owned the crop duster was tied up with complaints, but they had no idea what was happening. They were as confused as anyone else. The Black Sheet banner streaming from their plane was news to them. The pilot flying the plane with the banner promoting the Black Sheet did his regular run and returned to the airfield.

By this time, police cars, sheriff's cars, and even some private citizens had converged on and around the field, causing the pilot much consternation because he thought his boss had put the banner on the plane as usual. The pilot climbed out of the cockpit to a firestorm. He was just getting a good look at the banner, and he was surprised and dumbfounded.

When asked who attached the banner to his plane, all he could do was shrug his shoulders. It was a mystery to him. When asked why he didn't take it off, he admitted he didn't see it. It wasn't open. It must have been folded up tight, and the wind blew it open.

Morning coffee on the front porch was a perfect time for Oceans and Enoch to bond and talk about the banner they had just seen in the air. Hester was busy in the kitchen doing her morning chores and humming a spiritual. Like many others, she liked to keep up with the gossip on the party line, and every few minutes, she would pick up the phone and listen in. She was intrigued when she heard them talking about the Black Sheet. After listening awhile, she came to the front door to share the news with Enoch and Oceans.

"It's on the party line. White and colored folks are going crazy. You should hear them, something about a banner flying over the city."

Both Oceans and Enoch jumped up at the same time, almost tripping over each other and trampling Hester who barely got out of the way in time.

"Have you both gone crazy?" she screamed in frustration.

But they didn't hear her. They were both listening in excitedly on the telephone.

As many times as Enoch had teased her about listening to the party line and even called her a busybody, she couldn't believe he and her son were listening in. She just stood there a second gaping, not understanding what was happening. Enoch and Oceans could barely contain their excitement, but for different reasons. Enoch because colored people had an ally. Oceans because his banner was creating attention to Black Sheet.

All day long, people talked about the Black Sheet and the banner caper. Oceans went by Red's joint, and that was the main topic. The town of Caloosa was in a strange mood like the Black Sheet had eclipsed the city by obscuring the KKK, making it less outstanding. What's next was the question on everybody's mind. An unplanned alliance now existed between the forces against the Klan.

NEWSPAPER ARTICLE ABOUT FLYOVER

> People all over town were looking up at the banner with awe and disbelief. Is Black Sheet taking over our skies now? The crop duster flying over our city was pulling, of all things, a banner message from this plague of our society promising vengeance against the KKK. The nerve of this scoundrel actually advertising his defiance and contempt for authority. Is law enforcement doing enough to curtail this black-hearted culprit? Just asking.

Black people were outwardly thrilled and elated, but white people were up in arms and demanding that the police find and eliminate this self-appointed vigilante. Black folks, however, saw him as a champion for blacks in their struggle against the KKK, and maybe Jim Crow too.

SECOND LYNCHING THREAT

Victim

The old green station wagon was a familiar sight bouncing down the dirt road rattling and raising clouds of red dust. Silvester Jackson had just finished another long day's work, first in the cotton field where he picked his backbreaking consistent 250 pounds of cotton a day, an astounding amount of production outdoing every other picker in the cotton field, and then worked into the night doing odd jobs for the local white people. Everybody knew Silvester and called him big Sil. He was huge, over six-foot-four and 275 pounds of solid muscle, and he was gentle, a gentle giant. He had a wife (who weighed under 100 pounds) and eight kids and a widowed mother-in-law to support, and if he ever complained, nobody heard him. As if he didn't have enough to do, he and his wife, Annie, worked a sharecrop and out-produced most of his neighbors. No one could figure out when they found the time to make babies because he was always busy, yet she was always pregnant.

"Mrs. Tracy sent a note over. She got some work for you. She said it's urgent, and she needs you to come over first thing in the morning," his wife said as he stepped out of the car.

"Sunday? Did she say what it was?"

"She didn't say, but she said it wouldn't take long."

"Sometimes I wish I'd never taken work from the Tracys. They're too demanding, and they ain't never satisfied. Now they want me to work on a Sunday."

"Come on and eat your supper before it gets cold."

Mrs. Tracy was sitting in the porch swing when he drove up. "It's about time you got here," she complained. "Didn't Annie tell you I said it was urgent?" she said getting up and going to the door. "Come on in the house."

"Where's Mr. Tracy?" he asked, looking around as he started up the porch steps.

"He had to run over to Leesburg on business."

Hearing this, he stopped.

"I said come on in," she commanded.

"Well now, I don't think that's a good idea, me coming in and your man's not home."

"I said come on in. Are you sassing me?"

"No, ma'am. It just don't seem right." He had seen the strange way she looked at him sometimes, and he was starting to feel uneasy.

"Well, the work is inside, and you sure can't do it from out there."

Reluctantly, he went on into the house.

"In here," she said, walking into the bedroom.

He immediately became nervous. He knew he couldn't be caught alone with this white woman in her bedroom no matter how innocent it seemed.

"Come on in!"

"No, ma'am, that wouldn't be proper, a colored man alone in the bedroom with a white woman. Why, I'd be lynched." He thought it looked innocent enough, but it didn't feel right and decided that the smart thing to do was get out of the house now. He turned and started for the front door as fast as he could walk.

"Come back here!" she screamed, but he kept walking. "I said come back here."

By this time, he was at the screen door, and she was close behind yelling. "You can't do that to me and get away with it!"

Her husband had just walked up on the porch and was opening the door. Silvester bumped into him and knocked him off balance.

"What the hell is going on here?" he cried out. "Do what to you?"

Before he could say anything, she started screaming and screaming like she was being assaulted.

"Nothing, Mr. Tracy. I didn't do nothing." He didn't know what else to say or how to explain it; therefore, he just left.

Mrs. Tracy saw a chance to punish him for walking out, and she said, "He tried to rape me."

Silvester knew he had made a mistake the moment he walked out. He should have stayed and explained it. He started to get out of his car and go back when he heard Mr. Tracy say, "He did what? Tried to rape you?"

That's all Silvester heard, then he drove away as fast as he could. All he had done was refused to work in her bedroom without her husband being present, but if she said he had done something improper, he would be lynched without question.

He ended up at the Tires's place. Oceans and his father listened intently as he told what had happened.

"Better get home and be with your family, Sil," his father advised. "This is bad. I don't know whether to tell you to stay or to run."

Later that day, Oceans went by Red's to see if he could pick up any information about Silvester. Red rushed to the end of the bar as soon as Oceans came in.

"Boy, am I glad to see you," he whispered. "Somebody needs to warn Silvester Jackson."

"Why? What's happening?" Oceans asked, pretending ignorance of Silvester's dilemma.

"The Klan is going to pay him a visit tonight. He's been accused of trying to rape a white woman, and anybody who knows Sil knows that's a damn lie. I'd do it, but I can't get away from here right now."

"I'll get over there and tell him. Maybe, he can get out before they get there. Maybe that Black Sheet fellow will show up to help him if he doesn't," Oceans speculated."

"That's just what they want. They're using Silvester to set a trap for the guy in the black sheet. Word is they'll have two squads, one at the house and another hiding in the cornfield about forty yards away."

Silvester was frantic with worry about being lynched for nothing when Oceans got to his farm. His wife and kids were also in a frenzy.

"You've got to get out," Oceans said, wasting no time with preliminaries. "The Klan is coming."

"Ever . . . Everything we ha . . . have is he . . . here. We ca . . . can't ju . . . just le . . . leave!" Silvester was so mad that he was stuttering and slurring his words. "Th . . . that bi . . . bitch Li . . . Linda Tr . . . Tracy se . . . set me up, and I'm forced to leave everything I worked all my li . . . life for. I can't do it, Oceans," Silvester said, regaining some of his composure. "I just can't do it—not before killing some of those sons of bitches first."

"Maybe you can talk with them, make them understand. You didn't do nothing."

"You're talking crazy, Deborah. You can't reason with those animals."

"He's right," Oceans agreed. "They're not rational. They'll kill him on sight, then hang his body from the nearest tree. They're vicious and bloodthirsty, and they are cowards hiding behind white sheets. You can't stay here, Silvester. If they don't get you tonight, they'll get you another night."

"Where would we go?" Silvester's wife asked. "What would we do?"

"You'll live for one thing. You can figure the rest out later."

Silvester had been silent for a while, just listening. "He's right, you know—they'll believe what that woman told them. I hate to leave all of our hard work too, but I don't want to die for it, and I don't want to lose you. But! I am going to talk to them before I leave—in the only way they understand.

"Thanks for stopping by to warn us, Oceans. Now, you better get out of here while you can."

"Try to get your family out of here before they come," Oceans coaxed.

On impulse, Oceans put a few dollars of his back pay and a Black Sheet cutout into an envelope and stuffed it into the back seat of Silvester's station wagon. He hoped this money would help Silvester resettle his family somewhere up north.

Knowing that Wesley Simmons and his Klan was planning a surprise reception for Black Sheet, Oceans prepared for them. The fields on the west side of the main house were filled with lush corn over six feet tall. Oceans watched as three Klan pickup trucks loaded with Klansmen pulled into the cornfield to hide and wait.

This was the Klan members setting a trap for Black Sheet. About three hundred feet behind them was a fruit orchard peppered with apple, orange, pear, and pecan trees. That's where Black Sheet and his sniper rifle would be.

It was a perfect place to hide, with easy access to the cornfield without being seen. He couldn't have had a better spot even if he had built it himself. Two trees had grown together and formed in such a way that they formed a bulwark of roots above the ground. It was located at the highest point in the orchard. They wouldn't see him in the darkness. Now all he had to do was wait.

He was hoping Silvester would get his family out in time, but his last words implied that he would kill before he ran. A sudden rumbling sound coming from the road caught his attention. The sky was clear that so it couldn't be thunder. Then he saw the other Klan trucks coming down the lane headed for Silvester's house.

Several white men were in the trucks parked in the cornfield. From his vantage point, he could see their heads of the men in the trucks waiting in the cornfield. The Klan thought they were going to ambush him, and Black Sheet was going to show up just as they wanted, but they were in for a big surprise. He was going to ambush them.

Silvester stood by the door waiting. His station wagon was just outside the back door idling. The Klan trucks stopped right in front of the house. Unperturbed, he waited until the hooded figures started piling out of the trucks. He stepped out the door and started shooting, killing two and wounding another before they could scatter and find cover.

"I'll be damned!" one of the Klansmen screamed his surprise from behind a tree. "That nigger was just sitting there waiting for us. I thought this would be easy."

"Somebody help Casey! I think the others are dead!" a Klansman yelled.

"You help him! I'm not going out there."

"You just made it harder on yourself!" Scott Tracy shouted to Silvester from behind a truck.

"What are you going to do, lynch me twice?" Silvester roared back. Then he started shooting up the trucks so that they couldn't follow them when they left. The others started shooting, peppering the front of the house with rifle and gunfire.

"Come on out of there, nigger, or we'll kill your whole family!"

"I ain't coming out, and some of you ain't going home. You'll be dead. You thought it was gonna be easy. I may die, but I'm gonna kill me some honkeys before I go. You were going to kill me for nothing. Now, some of you are going to die for nothing."

"You call what you tried to do to my wife nothing!" Scott Tracy shrieked.

Loud laughter was his answer at first. "Mr. Tracy, all I tried to do to your wife was get away from her, and that wasn't easy."

For a while there was a tense standoff with neither side having an advantage. Suddenly there was a huge explosion in the cornfield. Black Sheet had sprung his surprise. The Klansmen in the cornfield were in shock. They didn't know what hit them. Some started to panic. One minute they were waiting for Black Sheet, and the next all hell broke loose. One truck was blown apart, and the Klansmen in there were dead. Several others were hurt, some in a daze milling around aimlessly.

"You men in the cornfield, get out of your trucks, drop your weapons, and go to the front of the house where I can see you," Black Sheet said through the bullhorn. "You have one minute before the next explosion.

"Mr. Jackson, hold your fire. You men shooting at the house, drop your weapons and step out in front of the house. I want all Klansmen in front of the house where I can see you."

The Klansmen walked meekly to the front of the house. The surprise explosion had completely unnerved them. They were scared, confused, and terrified.

The Klan had come as a mob to kill, not to be killed. The cowards were caught in their own trap. They had suffered a lot of loses already. The remaining Klan members were looking all around, trying to figure out where he was.

"Glad you could make it, fellows," he said through a bullhorn. "I'm right over here standing in the moonlight for all to see. I got here early and waited for you. See, I knew about your little trap. I was there. I can see everyone now, and I'd feel much better if you would take your hoods off. Just in case you didn't know it, I've got a friend down there standing in the shadows. Say hello to what's left of the Klan."

Using his skills in ventriloquism, Black Sheet sent a voice from the shadows.

"This going-away party just wouldn't be the same without Decker O'Connor, Jim Wallace, Elden Green, Richard White, and the rest of your comrades. Now, just in case I missed someone in the cornfield, I'm going to throw another grenade into that cornfield. If anyone is left in there, they're going to die, and if they live, it will be without arms or legs or maybe eyesight.

"Now, fellows, I want to welcome you all and thank you for coming. The reason we welcome you is to help this family with their moving expenses. Just throw your money through Mr. Jackson's window that you shot out."

"What? Is he crazy?" one of the Klansmen blurted. "I'm not giving that nigger a dime."

"I'm only going to ask you once, Mr. Tracy. Maybe you'd rather die. Oh! By the way, your wife was lying. Mr. Jackson didn't try to rape her. He was just trying to get the hell out of there before she attacked him. You should sic the Klan on her.

"Everybody who wants to live, take out your billfold and all of your money and hold it in your hands. Now go over to the house one at a time and drop it through the window. Anyone who fails to do that will be shot. It's only fair to tell you that I'm going to have my associate do a random search of one of you, and if that one still has his wallet or his money, I'm going to shoot all of you.

"Silvester, if either one of them fails to drop money into your house, let me know. Once you get the money, just go to your car and drive away and have a safe trip."

"Good job, men," he said after the family drove away. "Now you, men, listen to me. I want you to stop this lynching, maiming, and terrorizing of our colored citizens. They are people too, whether you believe it or not. They have as much right to live unmolested as you do. If you stop these raids, I will disappear, and you'll never see me again. You'll have nothing to fear from me. If you don't, I will come to your homes and blow them sky high. The sheriff can't help you—he can't watch everyone's house. For one thing, while he's watching your house, who's going to be watching his house? We know he's a Klansman too.

"By the way, I was just kidding about the search. Your vehicles are disabled, so you'll have to walk."

When they saw him throw the grenade, they dove for the ground and tried to burrow into the soil like groundhogs looking for a lair. When they stood up, Black Sheet had disappeared.

BLACK SHEET STRIKES AGAIN!

The infamous man in the black sheet and hood—now simply referred to as Black Sheet—has struck again, giving the KKK the worst defeat in their history. This time, he broke up a trap set by the Klan to capture or kill him, proving that he was at the secret meeting where the plans were made. He set off two horrific explosions, blowing up trucks and killing or wounding several Klansmen who waited in a surprise ambush. As if that wasn't enough, he shot and wounded two more of our prominent citizens seeking justice for an attempted assault on a white woman. This man is dangerous to both white and colored, and this newspaper pledges to fight him with all of our means. Any man who would turn against his own kind is completely unpredictable. We call on the mayor, police chief, district attorney, and all other city officials to join us in rooting this varmint out. Now, he has the audacity to threaten our homes and families if colored families continue to be terrorized. This menace has to be found and destroyed.

KLU KLUX KLAN HEADQUARTERS MYSTERIOUSLY BURNED TO THE GROUND!

This headline in the *Caloosa Times* shocked the little town of Caloosa. The rest of the story was even more shocking.

> Last night the headquarters of the local KKK chapter was burned to the ground. The fire department arrived in time to save it, but someone had secured the gates with heavy chains and padlocks. Thousands of dollars in equipment and supplies were destroyed—not to mention the building itself. According to the police, evidence was found on the scene pointing to Black Sheet. The act of blatant arson outraged the white population and put their maids and farm workers in the peculiar position of having to pretend empathy with them while in their hearts, they were celebrating and rejoicing. What Black Sheet does next is anybody's guess.
>
> Today the KKK is quietly holding an emergency meeting at the courthouse. The mayor—a grand dragon of the KKK—has again openly declared war on Black Sheet for all the good that does. Until we know the identity of this scoundrel, no amount of planning will lead to his apprehension.

PRECISION TRUCK AND TRACTOR PARTS

Now that they had all of their equipment, it was time for Oceans and Yeboa—Osei's son—to use the skills that Osei had taught them to make the shop pay. They went to work fixing and rebuilding truck and tractor parts such as tire rods, exhaust pipes, fuel tanks, crankshafts, axles, steering rods, and muffler pipes. It started slowly. No one wanted to use them because they were black even though they were the best and had the most modern equipment. They had to win their customers' trust, prove they could deliver what they promised. Their shop was made up of mostly modern equipment thanks to Oceans's army back pay.

Their reputation started to grow through word of mouth, and slowly their business grew. They were fast and efficient. They were able to hire a few of the experienced, skilled colored mechanics as their workload grew. At first, they didn't make any personal money. It all went back into operating the business. As Osei had preached to them, the white man couldn't take this knowledge from them and if they did good work people would flock to them.

The black mechanics they hired were able to gain experience on modern equipment that they otherwise wouldn't have. They didn't even know that some of the equipment existed. At great expense, they brought the first forklift to Caloosa, and every man learned to use it, a skill that very few colored men had. It would be of great use when they arrived in the north as most of them would.

REACTION TO THE CONFRONTATION AT SILVESTER'S HOUSE

People were reacting to this new force of good or evil—depending on their perspective—all over the city. In the white community, it was shock, anger, outrage, even fear.

In the colored community, it was joy, elation, gladness, hope, even suspicion. Whoever was interfering with the KKK was causing a firestorm.

At a meeting at Red's bar, several black men got together to discuss Black Sheet.

BLACK MISTRUST OF BLACK SHEET

"You all know me," Murell said, taking a sip of his beer. "I don't believe he's for real. It's some kind of white trick. I mean, why would some white man help us?"

"I understand how you feel, Murell. I felt the same way, but I was out in the woods near Silvester's house, and I saw this man shoot two white people and heard what he said. He warned the KKK to stop terrorizing colored folks. If this is some kind of trick, I fell for it."

"So far he seems to be acting on our behalf, so instead of being suspicious, let's support him and see what happens. Why look a gift horse in the mouth?"

CITY HALL MEETING

The mayor called another council meeting assembling all of the top officials and KKK leaders in the city and surrounding towns.

Oceans parked near the courthouse and watched the KKK members file in. Many of whom were people he knew from his childhood who had pretended to be in sympathy with the plight of the Negro. Some were young men his age whom he had fought or even played with as a child. This meeting exposed persons that he hadn't even suspected were members of the hate group. He finally drove away with a whole new perspective of the city he lived in.

The meeting started without the usual formalities or protocol. Andrew Bonaparte was the first one to speak.

"This Black Sheet is more dangerous than we first thought, and he's causing other colored people to get aggressive too. Silvester Jackson had the nerve to step out the door and shoot George and Fred as soon as we drove up without, and he would have shot the rest of us if we hadn't scattered."

"What about Black Sheet? I thought you had set a trap for him," the chief of police interrupted.

"We had. Decker, Jim, Elden, and a few others were hiding in the cornfield as planned, but before they could do anything, he threw a grenade into the cornfield and blew up our trucks, killing the men inside. He knew about the trap."

"You mean he's got explosives?"

"Ain't that what I just said? Furthermore, I think he's one of us. In fact, he may be sitting here right among us now. The last thing he said was, 'I'll see you at the meeting.' To add insult to injury, he forced us to finance that nigger Jackson's trip out of our own pocket. Never have I been so humiliated. This maniac robbed us."

"Robbed you? So there's more to it than just helping the Negros?"

"No! No. He made us give all of our money to that nigger who assaulted Mrs. Tracy. He called it helping them with their moving expenses. Then he insulted Mrs. Tracy by implying that she was the rapist."

"I wouldn't have done it!" someone shouted. "Not one penny would I have given up!"

"Then you would have been dead," Andrew stated. For the next two minutes, he just stood there looking at them. Then he stated, "We're going to stop this lunatic, and if you're in here, I'm putting you on notice. When we catch you, you're gonna die slow. You're going to suffer. I propose a reward of five thousand dollars be put out for information leading to his capture, and I'll put up the first thousand. For five thousand dollars, even the blacks will turn his ass in if they know who he is."

It didn't take long to get pledges for the balance of the reward. The meeting continued for the rest of the morning, but not much was accomplished because they were suspicious of each other.

"Oh yes. Don't forget. This man is armed with explosives."

SILVESTER'S REACTION

Out of danger and out of Mississippi, the Jackson family relaxed a little and reflected on the past few hours. They had left everything behind that they worked so hard for, but they still had their lives. Now it was time to concentrate on the future. There was money all over the floor where Silvester had carelessly thrown it after he picked it up off the floor.

"I guess we had better count that money. God knows we're going to need it. Better get rid of those wallets too while you're at it."

"My God," his wife blurted out. "There's over five hundred dollars here. If we're careful, this should help us get started up north."

"I don't know how we would have got away from the Klan if it wasn't for Black Sheet."

"I know."

"I didn't even believe that stuff about him until he showed up at our house."

Now that Black Sheet had intimidated the KKK a second time and exposed some of the prominent secret members, they had lost some of their invincibility. According to some of the colored bystanders hiding in the woods, Silvester had not stood idle when the KKK came to lynch him but had attacked them, killing Richard White who seemed so righteous that no one would have ever suspected him of being a member of the Klan and one other Klansman that they didn't know. Those black families that witnessed the confrontation would never forget it, especially the part where Black Sheet threw the grenades and made the Klan give Silvester the money for his trip.

The Klan didn't look so brave when they were the victims. They were just as scared as a colored man is when they come in the night. Black Sheet should have killed them all, they thought.

STOP BLACK SHEET NOW

The sudden appearance of Black Sheet was starting to worry some of the more conservative white citizens. They wanted to preserve the existing conditions and were fearful of anything that might lead to change. This white fool had to be stopped—whoever he was—and made an example of.

It was this kind of thinking that led to the assault and battery of a white man named Addison Whitmon. He was driving down Main Street when he witnessed the attack on an old black woman walking with a cane. She was unable to get off the sidewalk fast enough to suit a couple of young white boys, and they pushed her off. She lost her footing and fell into a puddle of water.

Addison stopped and helped her up then chastised the boys. A crowd started to gather, and someone accused him of being Black Sheet. The threats escalated then someone threw a brick, hitting him in the back. Other bystanders joined in and started to beat him unmercifully. By the time they stopped, he was near death.

Two days later, a man killed his neighbor—accused of being Black Sheet—and demanded his reward, which was denied because of lack of proof. Another man who was known to have a liberal attitude toward colored folks was turned in as Black Sheet but released when he proved that he wasn't even in town at the time of the attacks.

GROVER AND REGINA

Grover and Regina were high school sweethearts and had been inseparable for four years. Now they were graduating, and he had a scholarship to Lane College in Jackson, Tennessee, about 110 miles away. They wouldn't be able to see each other until the end of the year. They were spending their last night together in the local park where lovers went for privacy. They knew it was patrolled by the sheriff's office but decided to take the chance. The north edge of the park was covered with bushes and clusters of shrubs and bushy vegetation. It was like a wilderness, a perfect place to find some privacy.

They found a spot under some bushes in the dark and started hugging and kissing each other. His hands soon started to roam over her body, and at first, she let him continue, but soon he started to caress her breast, and then his hands slid under her dress. She continuously moved his hands and pushed them away.

"No," she whispered.

"Why not?" he whispered back. "I thought you loved me."

"I do," she said, "but I don't want to do this."

"Just this one time before I go," he pleaded and started stroking and feeling again. "I really need you."

"If you really loved me, you would be willing to wait," she pleaded.

Suddenly a bright light was shining on them, and when they looked up, there were two sheriff's deputies standing over them.

"Just look what we've got here," one of them said.

"Get up," the other one said. "You're both going to jail."

They marched them to the car and took them to the police station.

"Put him in that cell, and I'll put her around here with the other women." They kept him in the cell for over two hours before letting him go.

"Where's my girlfriend?"

"She's long gone. We sent her home."

Grover went by Regina's, and her mother and father said she hadn't been home. They thought she was with him. Now he was scared because she should have been home by now. He started to walk back toward the police station, looking and hoping to see Regina walking back. After a while, he saw a shadow staggering through a yard and fall. He ran over there, and it was his Regina.

Her clothes were in disarray. Her hair was mussed up. Her lips were swollen and arms scratched up. When he ran to her, she fell into his arms crying.

"They raped me," she whispered. "They all raped me."

His heart dropped when he heard those words. He knew it was his fault. He should have guessed. Now all he could do was hug her and cry with her.

They felt broken as they walked home, slowly crying all the way. What could he tell her family? How could he explain allowing this to happen while she was with him? They were in a daze, overwhelmed, completely in shock. Everything around them was in a haze. It wasn't real, but it was real, surreal but real.

The next morning, he left for Lane College, but the thrill was gone—gone up in the tragedy of deceit and brutal rape. He took his seat in the back of the Greyhound bus like a zombie and started talking to himself. He was still rambling when the bus arrived in Jackson, Tennessee, at the school, and somehow he made it through orientation, but the rape and the deputies never left his mind even for a second.

Now he remembered hearing them bragging about patrolling the park every night and hitting the jackpot, but it didn't register what they were talking about. So he thought nothing of it at the time. Regina probably wasn't the only one. No telling how long they had been doing this and getting away with it. Somebody had to do something about it, and here he was away at college while Regina was suffering alone.

They said classes would start day after tomorrow, and without thinking about it, he automatically headed for the bus stop for a return to Caloosa. He arrived back just before dark, slipped by his house and picked up a baseball bat and two ropes, then went straight to the park without being seen by anybody. He hid in the bushes near where the patrol car had parked the night before and waited.

The patrol car soon pulled up and parked, and the officers got out laughing. "Let's see if we can hit the jackpot again tonight," the older one said.

"I just love taking that black pussy. Let's split up and look for prospects and meet back at the car," the young one said with a leer on his face.

Grover didn't hesitate. The minute they separated, he started stalking the nearest one, came up on him from behind, and tapped him on the shoulder.

"Remember me?" He sneered then busted him in the head with the bat. He didn't stop beating him until he was a bloody pulp. He was completely out of control. He dragged him back into the trees where he had his ropes waiting. He tied the rope around his neck and threw it over a tree limb. Being over six feet tall and two hundred pounds, he had no problem pulling him until his feet were off the ground. Then clenching his mouth together to keep from throwing up, he castrated him.

Grover, barely maintaining control of himself, returned to the car to wait for the other deputy. If anyone had told him two days ago that he was capable of this, he wouldn't have believed it, but he was determined to finish—he couldn't let this go unpunished. He had to do it for all of the others who had suffered from these animals and at the same time send a message to the others.

The second deputy soon returned grinning. He was bragging even before he reached the patrol car. "Hey, Johnny," he called, excitement in his voice, "where are you? I hit the jackpot again. Let's go have some fun."

He never knew what hit him. "Yeah, let's have some fun," Grover whispered. Grover tied him up, gagged him, and positioned him so that when he woke up, he could see his partner hanging from the tree castrated then sat down and waited for him to come to.

When he woke up and opened his eyes and saw his partner hanging there, he tried to scream, but the gag stopped him. His eyes were about to pop out.

Grover stepped into the moonlight, standing over him and said, "Remember me?" and snatched the gag out of his mouth.

The deputy's eyes were as big as the full moon over head. "Please," he started begging, "it was all Jeff's idea. I didn't even touch her. Please don't kill me. I'll never do it again."

Grover showed him the same mercy that Regina had been shown then left him hanging there beside his partner with a sign around his neck, "Animals and Rapists!"

Back at the police station, the other two deputies were getting impatient, and one remarked, "I wonder what's taking them so long. I'm getting horny."

When it was time for their shift to end and the others still hadn't returned, they just went on home.

Grover calmly went to a white-only water fountain and washed the blood off him then took the night Greyhound back to school.

The bodies were found the next morning lynched and castrated. They each had a sign hanging around their necks that just said "animals."

The *Caloosa Times* headline the next day was THAT DAMN BLACK SHEET.

> Black Sheet has reached a new low. Two sheriff's deputies were found in the park lynched and castrated.

Something must be done, or no one will be safe in our streets. These were both family men.

The paper didn't mention the "animals and rapists" sign hanging around their necks. The news of the two deputies found lynched and castrated in the park had many different reactions. In the black community, elation, happiness, excitement, exhilaration, euphoria, relief, and jubilation.

Black mothers, fathers, and daughters rejoiced—and boyfriends who, like Grover, gave a damn.

In the white community, alarm, disbelief, depression, sadness, sorry, unhappiness. To their knowledge, no white man had ever been lynched, and they hoped that this was not the start of a new trend.

The real story came out of Chicago in the *Defender*. A week after the lynching, the *Chicago Defender* put out a special edition with the full story of the lynching and the reason. These men were the lowest of the low. They were systematically abducting and raping young black girls, even taking them back to the station where other deputies participated in the rapes. Black Sheet would have done the colored community a great service had he lynched the entire sheriff's department. This was the story that the *Caloosa Times* wouldn't tell. Sheriffs' deputies should keep it in their pants if they wanted to keep it.

Oceans and Enoch sat on the porch reading the *Defender* version of the story and sharing their opinions.

"Up till now, Black Sheet has only attacked the Klan, and he hasn't lynched anyone," Enoch argued. "I don't believe he lynched those deputies. Do you, son?"

"I don't either. I think they're blaming Black Sheet because they don't know who did it."

"Then who? Who could have done such a gruesome thing?"

"I'd say somebody pretty angry or hurt. There's a story behind this, Pop, and I would really like to know what it is."

"I guess it's something we'll never know."

"The newspaper is blaming it on Black Sheet, and that's a good thing because they think Black Sheet is white, so it takes the heat off the black community."

Red's was unusually crowded for a Thursday night. People who didn't usually come out during the week had showed up at Red's to share and pick up the latest information and rumors about Black Sheet.

"I don't believe he's for real," a doubtful black farmer expressed his feelings of uncertainty and distrust. "It's just too good to be true. It's a trick."

"If it's a trick, it's in our favor," a true believer countered.

FAIR GROUNDS RUBY [97] DOWN

The crowd at the Fair Grounds was overflowing. This was one of the few forums where colored and white were allowed to mingle. All of the facilities were still segregated, but blacks had access to most everything else. Of course, many of the attendees segregated themselves.

Oceans walked through the photo gallery to the book concession, and a book by Alexandre Dumas caught his eye. The picture on the cover looked black, and that intrigued him even more. He was starting to remember a French black writer that one of his buddies in France had told him about who wrote a book called *The Three Musketeers*.

"Fancy meeting you here," a voice from behind him interrupted his musing, "and in my favorite section."

He turned to see if that familiar voice was addressing him, and to his surprise and happiness, Ruby was standing there with a big grin on her face.

"I was just thinking about you." He smiled back."

"Liar,", she cooed.

"Well, not right this minute, but off and on every day."

"What were you thinking?"

"There's a dance coming up, and I'd like to take you."

She smiled. "I'd like that. I heard about it, and I was hoping you would ask. By the way, what kind of books do you like?"

"I like all kinds. Right now I'm looking at *The Three Musketeers.*"

"That's a good one. That French writer is half-colored, you know."

"I thought I saw some color in his face."

Time passes fast when you're having fun; they had a great day.

"Come on, and I'll take you home," he offered. "Don't forget about Friday. I'll pick you up around eight."

REHIRE REFUSAL

"Betsy, girl, I been looking all over for you."

"You couldn't have looked too hard. Since I got fired, I'm real easy to find. I must have the cleanest house in the neighborhood 'cause I spend most days right here cleaning it."

"Well, maybe you'll be working again soon."

"You must know something I don't know."

"Your old boss, Mrs. Corbett, stopped me at the bus stop and told me to tell you to come by there. She wants to talk to you."

"What the hell do she want?"

"Probably wants you to come back."

"Well, you just tell her if she wants to see me, she can come by my house."

"Have you lost your mind? That white woman ain't gonna come to yo house."

"Well, she ain't no better than I am. Just tell her what I said."

"You may be crazy, but I ain't. I'll tell her I didn't see you."

Two days later, Betsy was sitting on her front porch swing when a car drove up, and Mrs. Corbett got out.

"Afternoon, Betsy," she said just like they were friends or something.

"Hi, Shirley," she answered just like they were friends or something. "What brings you out this way?"

Mrs. Corbett hesitated a second at the familiarity then said, "I wondered if you'd like to have your job back."

"No, thank you, Shirley. I've decided to retire."

"I admit I may have been a little hasty in firing you, and I know you need the work, so why are you being stubborn about coming back?"

"You said you didn't want no smart-ass nigger working for you, and I don't want to work for no dumb-ass white woman."

"You can't talk to me like that."

"I just did."

Mrs. Corbett was silent for a few seconds and then surprised Betsy. "I swallowed my pride when I came over here and again when I let a colored woman talk to me like that. It's easy to replace you as a cleaning woman, but my girl's been getting better grades since you helped her, and that's not easy for me to say. I've been looking down at you, and I'm sorry. I didn't know Negroes could be that smart. I still want you to come back."

Betsy just looked at her for a minute and said, "If it means that much, I'll be there tomorrow."

CHAPTER 8

Sniper Attack

Oceans was facing a dilemma. He knew he was going after the KKK, and he couldn't sit around waiting for them to lynch another colored man.

That night, he paced the floor in his room, trying to decide what to do next. In front of his father that morning, he had seemed so sure of himself. But in reality, he was doubtful. He wanted to be bold but not reckless. Getting caught and lynched was a possibility he didn't want to chance. He went to bed still undecided what to do, but his subconscious couldn't rest.

His answer came in the middle of the night. Sniper rifle. He could use it to harass Klansmen in their homes. He didn't even have to go close to the place, just sit back 500 yards and shoot the building to pieces and be gone before anyone could figure out where he was.

He planned his sniper attack for the very next day, and as luck would have it, an emergency meeting about Black Sheet was in progress. The parking area was loaded with cars and trucks, and right up front by the door, he saw the mayor's / grand dragon's city vehicle.

Hello, mayor, I'm glad you're here, he said to himself as he put a few rounds into the mayor's car before starting on the building and the rest of the vehicles. He proceeded to shoot out windows and doors and signs and tires and windshields. He had a perfect spot in a stand of woods about 500 yards away. Nobody came out or tried that he could see.

Now you know how colored folks feel when you come around burning crosses and shooting and threating people, he said in his mind. The whole attack was over in less than five minutes, and he calmly went back to his car.

Confused thoughts raced through his mind as he drove away. What had his life become? Before he joined the army, he would have never done this. Now he was a man starting a war after just fighting in one. His alter ego, Black Sheet, was being sought by the KKK and also scared white citizens. He could be unmasked at any time and endanger not just his family but all colored families in the city as well. Yet here he was attacking the Klan's new headquarters, and for what? They were a plague on the colored race—that's what. They lynched one of his childhood friends and killed and maimed with impunity. Somebody had to do something, and that somebody was Black Sheet because he could pass for white and do it without starting a race war. The fallout from this would determine his next move.

BIG KKK RALLY AGAINST BLACK SHEET

According to Mayor Wesley Simmons, grand dragon of the KKK, the latest Black Sheet incident is bringing the KKK out in force to fight against it. They have vowed to find the white traitor in the black sheet and kill him at all cost. Klan chapters from all local towns are converging on the city as a show of support to stop this menace once and for all. It is believed by doctors that this person is mentally disturbed and dangerous to themselves and others around him. If anyone has the least suspicion of the culprit's identity, contact the mayor's office immediately. You will remain anonymous. The sooner this threat is eliminated, the safer the whole community will be. This Klan spectacle is projected to be over 1,000 strong.

Oceans read this article that appeared in the *Caloosa Times* with interest. He knew that what he was thinking was foolhardy and dangerous, but he intended to be at that rally passing out his calling cards. The rally was a week away, so he had plenty of time to get ready.

He spent the next few days cutting paper dolls from black crepe paper in the image of the Black Sheet. He also made a few small flyers with the message YOUR DEMISE IS NEAR. DON'T MAKE ANY PLANS FOR THE FUTURE and sighed it "Black Sheet." The last thing he did was make sure he had a clean white Klan robe and hood for the big day. The one thing that he knew for sure was if he was discovered, he was dead.

There was one other thing that he wanted to do before the big rally. That night, he found a perfect spot to deliver a message to covert (closet) members of the KKK. From 500 feet away, he shot out the windows of seven covert Klansmen.

OCEANS AND HIS FATHER ONE ON ONE

They sat there on the porch making small talk and enjoying a father-and-son moment, the second one since Oceans returned home from the war. It was just before noon, and a grasshopper caught their attention as he tried to get away from a determined bird looking for lunch. Oops, he didn't make it. A line of worker ants busy following each other to and from a destination under the ground distracted them for a moment.

"Oceans, have you read the Caloosa paper today?" Enoch asked, breaking the silence.

"Yeah, Dad, I read it."

What do you think of the Klan rally against Black Sheet?"

"I hadn't really thought about it, Dad."

"They're looking for him so they can lynch him. They think he's someone they know, and they've got everyone on alert."

"Well, I, for one, hope they never catch him."

"We all do. I was thinking there must be some way we can help him. Maybe we could all get some black sheets and hoods and do some terrorizing ourselves, you know, like a Black Sheet Klan. As long as we don't say anything, they won't know we're black. We'd just be some more white folks helping blacks. I know it sounds crazy, but I just want to do something."

"It's too dangerous, Dad. If one of us got caught, he'd tell on everybody else, and they would come through the colored section like locusts, killing and burning and lynching men, women, and children. It's a good idea, but it's too big a risk. Maybe there's some other way we can help. Let's think about it."

"Well, we'd better think fast because that Klan gathering is only a week away, and there's no telling what they're planning."

"Let's not rush into anything, Dad. The Black Sheet seems to be doing okay so far. Let's just stay out of his way."

BLACK SHEET ATTENDS KLAN MEETING

The sunlight streaming through his window woke him up bright and early on the morning of the Klan rally. He threw off his sheet and rolled out of bed yawning. He washed up, emptied his bladder, put on his jeans, and went to the shed for his disguise—this time a white sheet and hood instead of the black. He would still be Black Sheet, but he just wouldn't look like it. He had the Black Sheet cutouts that he had cut the day before.

Oceans was up and out of the house right after breakfast the day of the Klan meeting. He was nervous, but he figured a sea of white sheets was enough to hide one. He also figured they wouldn't be expecting the Black Sheet to be dumb enough to attend. Besides, even if they caught him, he would just be a black man attending the Klan rally. They wouldn't know he was Black Sheet because they thought Black Sheet was a white man.

As he approached the downtown area, he noticed that the whole town seemed to be in a festive mood. Whole families were gathered on the side of the street, cooking and laughing and joking and having a holiday. Banners were flying, flags with the insignia of the KKK were waving, Confederate flags streaming, balloons were bobbing, grills were smoking, and leaflets had been distributed, and some littered the street. Vendors were spread out along the parade route down Main Street and up Fair Street all the way to the Fair Ground where the rally was to be held. Hawkers were on each corner, selling their wares and singing the praises of the KKK. Some even had the gall to call them Knights of the Ku Klux Klan. Knights! Did they really think these haters and butchers were noble or honorable or exalted? Knights! They were more like common, lowborn, and ignoble. Homemade beer, wine, and bootlegged liquor were flowing, and white sheets were everywhere.

Oceans had walked right down Main and Fair Streets, white sheet flapping around his legs. Today he was one of them, just another member of the Knights of the KKK, but for him, it was a masquerade. But this masquerade could get him killed if someone snatched off his hood. But even if they discovered he was black, they wouldn't know he was Black Sheet.

A couple of the Klansmen looked at him long and hard as he approached them, and he was afraid that they suspected something. But the moment passed, and he kept walking as if he belonged, paying them no attention. Nobody challenged him as he mingled around the fairgrounds, discretely leaving his Black Sheet cutouts and leaflets on chairs and tables and even on the platform that was set up for the speakers.

The imperial wizard—a national officer who had made a special trip to support the local agenda—the grand dragon, the highest-ranking Klansman in the state, and his officers arrived while Oceans was in the fairground, and all of the attention was drawn to them. The imperial wizard had laid a stack of papers on a table that was reserved for him and went to shake hands with the grand dragon. In a daring and dangerous move, Oceans placed a few cutouts and a stack of leaflets on top of the imperial wizard's papers and quickly moved away from the table.

Slowly, he drifted back toward Fair and Main Streets, leaving a few of his leaflets on the street as he made his way away from the rally. He had almost made it all the way to the edge of town before he heard the first commotion. It sounded like it came from the fairgrounds, but he couldn't be sure.

The imperial wizard sat down at his table, and the grand dragon handed him his speech about the Black Sheet menace. This trip, he felt, was more of a nuisance than a necessity, but an election was coming up soon, and he wanted to keep his position and the perks that went with it. He believed in his own mind that somebody had panicked, and the whole thing had been blown way out of proportion, but since this chapter seemed concerned, he would—

The imperial wizard gasped and jumped out of his seat, spilling his drink, knocking over his chair, and dumping papers everywhere. He barely kept his balance. Looking around wildly, his face beet red, he stumbled away from the table. His chief of staff and his bodyguards, concerned at his sudden outburst, rushed to his, side thinking something must have been terribly wrong.

"H-he's here!" He gulped, looking all around him. "He's here."

"Who's here?" the chief of staff asked, not understanding.

"That damn Black Sheet!" he shrieked, handing the papers to his chief of staff. "He's around here somewhere! Find him!"

The grand dragon, who was usually pretty composed, became hysterical mostly because he was embarrassed. By this time, other Klan members had crowded around the table and adjoining area, wondering what was wrong.

"Where did you get these?" the sheriff asked in a demanding voice.

"It was on top of my speech when the grand dragon handed it to me," the imperial wizard rasped. "The Black Sheet was right at my table. He could still be here. He could be anyone."

Pandemonium broke out. The dragon's bodyguards were detaining and searching everybody nearby. Hoods were snatched off. Spectators were questioned and roughed up. Klansmen had to prove their identity. Now leaflets and Black Sheet cutouts were being found all over the street. Word went through the street that Black Sheet was in the crowd. People were looking at each other with suspicion even if they knew them. Fights broke out. People were running and pushing each other.

It was a riot. Peace couldn't be restored until Black Sheet was identified and captured.

"I saw him walking around passing out leaflets, and he had something black in his hands. He was dressed like a Klansman. I thought something was funny because he looked like he was leaving and the rally hadn't even started."

A man a few steps away had just picked up a Black Sheet leaflet and was putting it back down.

"That's him! That's him there! The man putting the leaflet down. Don't let him get away."

He started to run, but the other Klansmen surrounded him before he could get away.

"I'm not Black Sheet!" he cried. "You got the wrong man."

"Then why did you run?" someone asked?.

"I didn't know what else to do."

They didn't give him a chance. They just started beating him with bricks and sticks and kicking and stomping him and would have killed him if the grand dragon hadn't stopped it. He wanted to make an example of him.

Enoch woke up soon after Oceans left for the fairgrounds. He had a taste for a breakfast of hot fried catfish, and they were biting like mad down at the bayou. He called Oceans several times, and he didn't answer.

"Let him sleep," Hester called. "He's probably tried."

"Tired of what?" Enoch called back. "He ain't done nothing." He pushed open the bedroom door and started inside. "Get out of that bed, and let's go catch us some fish." Then he noticed that Oceans's bed was empty. "Damn, he's up and out already," he chuckled and turned to leave the room when something on Oceans's desk caught his eye.

He walked over for a closer look and saw a Black Sheet cutout. Then he saw some carefully printed leaflets by the pillow. His heart started to pound, and sweat beaded on his forehead. He thought about how Oceans had been acting lately like there was something on his mind.

Then the black-dye incident came to mind, and when he asked him why he needed black dye, he just shrugged it off.

The white man helping blacks that no one could understand, and he was indifferent to. His ability to mimic voices precisely. He should have seen it long before now. Oceans was the mysterious Black Sheet! Black fool was more like it. He was going to get himself killed, and where in the hell was he now.? Then he remembered the big Klan rally today over at the fairgrounds, and suddenly he knew.

That boy had lost his mind. He had a death wish. The war had effected his reasoning. He walked out to the porch and looked down the lane leading to the house, hoping to see Oceans driving down the lane, but he saw nothing. He sat down and began to worry.

Hester stepped out on the porch and was surprised to see him still there. "I thought you and Oceans were going fishing this morning. I've got a craving for fried catfish myself, especially the way you fry it."

"Oceans had to make a run. I'm waiting for him to come back now."

"Oh? I didn't hear him drive away."

"He was already gone when I got up."

"Is something wrong, Enoch? Did you and Oceans have an argument or something?"

"No, everything is fine. Everything is fine."

"Everything is not fine. Something is wrong, and don't tell me different. I know you."

"Just drop it, Hester. I said everything is fine."

She was quiet for a moment, but he knew that wasn't the end of it.

His mind drifted back for a moment to Oceans's childhood. By the time he was sixteen years old, Oceans was five-foot-ten and about 195 pounds, a formidable figure. He was coal black, and when he dressed up, his mother said he looked like an African prince. An inch shorter than his friend John Henry and two inches taller than Ben, he had powerful legs and arms and a thick neck. He walked with a confident swagger and carried himself with confidence. He had been heavily influenced by his African friend and mentor, Osei Obiri. He wanted to be like the Ashante solders—proud and brave.

That's why he was doing this—he had pledged to himself that he would fight to the death before he would stand idle and be lynched.

He didn't like to be called colored because he was coal black, and unlike many of his peers, he embraced his blackness. He had a little, sparse fuzz above his lip and the beginnings of a beard. His hazel eyes made him look menacing.

Oceans, John Henry, Ben, and Kenny were inseparable. They were like brothers. If you saw one, you knew the others were close by. They had a hate for the white establishment that was all-consuming.

"Why do we let white folks treat us like slaves?" Oceans asked one day while he and John were walking home from school. "We're as good as they are. There's a white boy fifteen years old working at the restaurant with me washing dishes just like me, and they pay him three times what they pay me and had enough nerve to tell me he's in charge."

"That's bull shit and you know it," John said.

"I know it, and everybody else knows it. I bust my ass for pennies while he makes dollars, and my father says I'm lucky to have a little job working inside, out of the hot sun."

"I have to agree with him on that one," Ben said. "I'm working outside slopping hogs, pulling weeds, chopping down trees, and anything else Mr. Redmond can find."

"I'm not talking about the work or working inside or outside. I'm talking about being treated like less than human. When I see my father stepping off the sidewalk to let a honky pass or my mother being disrespected by some white man, it makes me mad. The other day, the insurance man came to collect and didn't even knock. He just walked on in like he lived there and even went to the icebox and got some lemonade. I'm sick of this shit, and one day I'm going to explode."

Oceans had told him about that day, and he almost cried. Now Ben was gone, no, not gone, dead, lynched, and Oceans had lost his mind.

Hester interrupted his thoughts and brought him back to the present. "That must be Oceans coming back," she said pointing to a speeding car coming down the lane. "He's in an awfully big hurry. Something must be wrong."

"That's not Oceans's car. That's a truck. I think it's John Henry."

"Wonder why he's in such a hurry," Hester pondered.

"I'll go see what he wants," Enoch said, getting up and walking off the porch. "We'll know soon enough the way he's driving."

John was talking before his truck came to a complete stop. "Is Oceans here?"

"No, you haven't seen him?"

"I haven't seen him since Ben's funeral."

"Well, what's wrong? What are you so excited about?"

"Haven't you heard? Black Sheet showed up at the Klan rally. All hell broke loose—excuse my French, Mr. Russell—"

"That ain't French, John."

"They're killing each other up there looking for him."

"Did they catch him?" Enoch asked, afraid of the answer.

"Yeah, but not before a lot of people got hurt. Last I heard, they had beat him half to death until the grand dragon stopped it. Now I think they're going to ham string him and lynch him."

Enoch suddenly got lightheaded, and his legs got weak, and he started to fall. He caught himself by grabbing the door handle. John saw him falling and grabbed his arm to steady him. "Are you all right, Mr. Tires?"

Hester rushed down from the porch when she saw him falling.

"I'm all right. Just got dizzy for a minute, that's all."

"You better lay down for a minute anyway, honey. I'll get you some water."

"I'm fine now, really." He closed his eyes, and the memories started flooding back again.

It was the summer of 1941, and Oceans had just turned eighteen and, like many other colored men his age, joined the army. He fought back the tears as he waved to them from the Greyhound bus as it slowly pulled away. World War 2 had opened up opportunities to get away from the crunch of Jim Crow laws. Oceans was headed for Camp Shelby near Hattiesburg, Mississippi. He was still in Mississippi, but he was in the army now and away from the oppressive, smothering Jim Crow rules. He remembered how glad he was to see his son get away from the constant danger of saying or doing something that would get him lynched or imprisoned and put a road gang.

Oceans was so wild and unpredictable in those days, and from the looks of things he hadn't changed. If only he had realized Oceans was Black Sheet sooner, maybe he could have talked him out of it though he doubted it. The image of his son being caught and lynched was too much to bear, and he groaned involuntarily, causing Hester to grow concerned again. Now he wondered how he would break it to her.

"Here, drink this water, Enoch," Hester insisted for the third time. "You'll be all right in a minute. Jesus, another visitor coming. Who is it this time, I wonder.

"It drives like Kenny. He's the only one I know that drives that slow."

"I thought Kenny was gone back to the navy."

"He's not leaving until tomorrow."

A few minutes later, Kenny Branch pulled up to the house. "Hey, Mr. Tires, man, you're missing all of the fun."

"What fun?"

"The big Klan rally at the fairground. That Black Sheet fellow showed up, and all hell broke loose. They beat up a lot of Klansman looking for Black Sheet, and a lot of spectators got hurt. They caught Black Sheet and beat him to a pulp then lynched him. He turned out to be a Klan member. They—"

"Wait a minute, Kenny. Did you say he was a Klan member?"

"Right, one of their own people, and they treated him worse than they treat us. That's the part I like. They don't care who they kill."

"Wait a minute, Kenny. Slow down. You didn't happen to see Oceans anywhere, did you?"

"Just saw him up by Red's place talking to Young Blood."

"How long ago did you see him?"

"I saw him about twenty minutes ago, I guess."

"Are you sure about that, Kenny? You just saw him?"

"That's why I came by here. I thought he would be home by now."

"That looks like him coming now Kenny."

"Thanks, Mrs. Tires."

As Oceans approached the house, he saw his father looking down the road with a very relieved look on his face while his friend Kenny looked on smiling. Enoch met Oceans on the porch steps and gave him a big hug and whispered in his ear, "I was very worried and afraid for you, son."

"Why, Pop? I just went for a ride downtown."

"Don't try to deceive me anymore, son. We need to talk," he said, giving him another big hug.

"What's up, Pop?" Oceans, said frowning his confusion. "Kenny, man, I just left your house. Your mommy said you were over here. Are you still thinking about going back in the navy?"

"I'm leaving next week, and I asked Eline to marry me."

"I wondered when you were going to pop the question. Hell, man, you've been together since high school. What did she say?"

"She's ready to go with me now, but I told her to wait."

"Well, congratulations," Enoch and Oceans said in unison.

"Oceans we need to talk now."

"Okay, Pop."

"Have you heard about the dance at the Grand Ballroom tonight?"

"Yeh. I'm taking Ruby Asbrerry. Why don't we go together?"

"Oceans, we need to talk."

"Give me a minute, Pop."

"Me and Eline will pick you up at nine o'clock."

"The four of us crowd into the front of that truck? No thanks."

"Well then, you pick us up, Oceans!"

"Okay, Kenny, pick you up at nine. Let me go talk to my dad before he bust a gut."

After John and Kenny left, Enoch followed Oceans to his room. "Talk to you a minute, son. According to Kenny, Black Sheet showed up at the Klan rally and caused a riot."

"That's what I heard too."

"Did you hear that they caught him and lynched him?"

"Yeah, according to Young Blood, he was a Klan member. You just never know, do you, Pop?"

"I guess he fooled all of his friends and his relatives too," Enoch added. "What do you think they're going to do when they find out they lynched the wrong man?"

"Who said they lynched the wrong man?"

"Nobody yet, but when the real Black Sheet shows up, they're going to know unless you don't think the real Black Sheet is going to show up again."

"What are you trying to say, Pop?"

"I'm asking your opinion. Do you think the real Black Sheet is going to show up again?"

Oceans just stood there and looked at his father for a minute before he answered, "Okay, out with it, Dad. How long have you known?"

"Since this morning. I came in here to wake you up and saw the stuff on your bed, but I should have put it together sooner considering your talent for voices."

"Now I understand the big hug on the porch. When you heard the Black Sheet had been lynched, you thought it was me?"

"Yes, and it almost killed me."

"I'm sorry, Dad."

"So what's next, son? How long can you keep this charade up before you really get caught?"

"I'm going to keep it up until I discredit the KKK, put fear into the membership by terrorizing them right in their homes and on the scene every time they participate in a lynching."

"Haven't you already done enough, son? They're going to look like fools when people find out they lynched a perfectly dedicated white Klansman. That's gonna make the others feel insecure and the grand dragon look inept."

"I found out who led the group that killed Ben, and I'm going to kill him if I can."

"I'll help you all I can, but we've got to keep this from your mother. If she finds out, she'll worry herself to death. I know you won't listen, son, but now would be a good time for you to end this."

"I can't, Pop."

"Everybody thinks Black Sheep is dead. Bury him and be done with it. You know I don't approve of this."

"Sorry, Pop, but there's too much left to do. However, I feel your concern."

"Do you? I'm scared for you, son. That black sheet you wear don't make you bulletproof or lynchproof."

"I know, Dad, but I just can't stop now."

"Aren't you afraid? Tell me, son, how did you feel walking between all those white sheets?"

"I felt like a turkey at Thanksgiving. My knees were shaking so hard that I could barely walk. To tell the truth, Pop, I was so scared that I was having illusions of hanging from every tree on the parkway. But I tell you what, Pop, I don't think there's any need for Black Sheet to show himself again. He can still make his presence felt.

"I have a question, Pop. How did we get to this point? We were freed by the Emancipation Proclamation in 1863, which meant we were no longer in bondage. Yet the only difference between slavery and now is that instead of having one master, all white folks are our masters. They control every move we make, tell us where we can go and where we can't. They even put a curfew on how long we can stay out. We are little more than their possessions. The KKK is a self-appointed vigilante force that delivers punishment for perceived black crimes, but not justice. This punishment is actually terrorizing to keep us in our so-called place. Black Sheet wants to make them think twice—no, make them petrified to deliver that punishment. Until that's done, his job is not finished."

CHAPTER 9

The Dance

Oceans picked Ruby up at eight. It was their first date, and he was looking forward to it. He had never met her family and wanted to make a good impression. He had on black baggy cuffed pants over shiny gray shoes and a gray striped shirt with a black vest that he had picked up in New York during a stopover on his way home. He had worn this outfit to a dance at the Savoy in Harlem where he learned the jitterbug.

It was a hot night, so the family was sitting on the front porch when he pulled up out front. After all he had been through, he couldn't believe he was feeling like a scaredy-cat. He actually had butterflies in his stomach as he walked up the brick sidewalk toward the front porch to run the family gauntlet. Everything was exaggerated. The crickets sounded like a small army in his ears.

"Evening, Mr. and Mrs. Asberry, my name is Oceans Tires, and I'm here to pick up Ruby."

"Ruby!" her mother yelled. "Your date is here."

"Okay, Momma."

Her brothers and sisters were staring at him as he waited. Then Ruby stepped out of the screen door, and he was awe-struck. She was wearing a just-below-the-knees form-fitting skirt with a wide belt and a silk blouse tucked in. Her shoes had a low heel with a strap, and her hair was pulled back in a ball with a ribbon.

They picked up Kenny and his date who already knew Ruby, and they laughed like little children all the way to the dance.

The dance was already jumping when they got there. The jitterbug was swinging. The music was blasting, and the partyers were already swaying and gliding with the music. Oceans and Ruby jumped right in and spent the next hour doing the jitterbug, jive, the Lindy hop, and the rumba. Then the DJ slowed it down so the people could rest up with a little slow drag.

"Where did you learn all of that?" he asked as he took her in his arms.

"I learned it at school. How about you? I thought you just got out of the army."

"I stopped in New York on the way home and spent a few nights in Harlem at a place called the Savoy Ballroom. They do it all there." He held her close as they glided across the floor. His right hand was low on her back, his left hand at his side. Then he pulled her into a closed embrace and stopped moving, doing a slow grind in one place.

Ruby rolled her hips twice in a controlled grind just to let him know that she was game then backed off to signal "but not now." She swung out and led him into a side-by-side walk.

"I thought I was leading this dance," he whispered.

"When a man leads in the wrong direction, a woman has to take the lead," she whispered back.

"I had to try," he whispered.

"I got your message. Did you get mine?" she whispered again, then they both laughed, did a breakaway, some turns, improvised some footwork, and he threw in some backward loose-leg movements, and they both headed for the bar where Kenny and some other friends were hanging out.

From the time he picked Ruby up, the night was magic. The band seemed to be playing just for them. By the time it was over, he was spellbound.

"Can you come by my church tomorrow?" she asked as he was driving her home.

"What church do you go to?"

"New Philadelphia on the Pike."

"Do you have to go right home after church.?"

"I got to catch the three-o'clock Greyhound to Jackson. I just came home for the dance."

"I'll take you back to school."

When they pulled up to the school, the next day, Ruby saw her French professor coming down the sidewalk. "Oh, there's my French professor. Salut comment allez-vous," she greeted him. (Hello, how are you?)

"Jevais blen merel," he answered. (I'm well, thank you.)

"Jene te connais pas mais je suis content que tu te de brouvilles bien." (I'm fine, thank you very much. I'm glad you are doing well.)

Ruby and her professor were so surprised that they were speechless for a while.

THE MEETING

CALOOSA TIMES

The KKK rally at the fairgrounds was the scene of Black Sheet making a daring attempt to cause chaos by showing up in his KKK regalia to pass out cutouts. Too bad for him he didn't anticipate the quick and decisive action of the grand dragon who was in attendance. As soon as he saw the material, he initiated a search and caught him red-handed before he could escape. What is this city coming to when we find out one of our most respected citizens is working against us on behalf of the coloreds? His family says that the wrong man was killed and that Bob Horton wouldn't help a black man. If they're right, this would be the biggest blunder in Caloosa history, and the grand dragon would be responsible. But there's little chance of there being a mistake since there was an eye witness who said he saw him passing out Black Sheet propaganda materials while wearing his KKK paraphernalia. Of course, it is tragic that so many innocent spectators were beaten and injured during the process of ferreting out this traitor to the white cause. We consider him the very lowest of the low. He even fooled those closest to him. Even his closest friends are now speaking out against him. The only positive thing that came out of this is that the Black Sheet has been caught and killed. Now the city can return to normal and hopefully forget about the Black Sheet.

The next day, the newspaper came out with another exposé article changing its tune.

Based on a message just received from someone calling themselves Black Sheet, we have reason to believe that the man brutally killed at the rally yesterday was not Black Sheet. We are investigating. Additional information to follow.

Too late they found out that they lynched the wrong man.

An innocent man whom they thought had been Black Sheet has been lynched even though he screamed his innocence. Not only that, but he had been a white Klan member with a family in good standing lynched without a trial. So what did the eyewitness really see, and how does he feel after identifying the wrong man? Maybe he was Black Sheet and was passing the buck. He has since disappeared.

More on this later.

There was no sympathy at all in the colored community. They had seen this injustice too many times to friends and relatives. The city leaders didn't know what to do or who to blame. The only thing they could agree on was that they had to catch Black Sheet. The newspaper was playing the incident up big, which just fueled the firestorm.

> Several of our most prominent citizens had their homes peppered with bullets last night, proving that Black Sheet is alive and well, and this newspaper found a message under our door this morning. We are printing the message word for word for the benefit of our readers.
>
> Like Lazarus, Black Sheet rises again—this time with a vengeance. Next time a colored man is lynched or threatened, I'm going to visit each Klan member at his home. Only this time, I won't be aiming at the house. You won't see me but you'll feel me. B.S.
>
> In the opinion of this newspaper, this message is genuine. This paper believes that the wrong man was lynched, and Black Sheet is still alive.
>
> The Grand Dragon owes Bob Houston's wife and children more than he can ever pay. Too bad he can't bring their father and husband back.

"As descendants of African people who were brought to America against our will and as slaves, we inherited a lifetime of injustice, but it's time for us to reject that inheritance."

Wesley Simmons, as a grand dragon, was very outspoken in his views about keeping the colored in their place. To him, that meant controlling every part of their lives. They were less than human and should be treated that way. The Jim Crow laws were too lenient, he warned. Even with separate bathrooms, separate water fountains, separate schools, they had too much. "They should have never been emancipated," he often complained. "Send them back to Africa" was his mantra. But his mouth was his Achilles' heel. His friends had grown tired of hearing him complain about the Negro even though some of them felt the same. Mostly there was a fear that because of the maltreatment of the Negro, there would be a revolt.

It was a council meeting called to discuss the Black Sheet menace, and most of the town leaders were there. They were in the middle of considering a plan to trap and capture or kill him. Ideally, capturing him and making an example of him was the preference. The chief of police was speaking when the door suddenly opened and Black Sheet stepped into the room.

"This is my only warning. If you continue to terrorize the Negro community, you will all die!" he said, backing out of the room and closing the doors behind him.

He quickly secured the doors with a rod through the handles, pulled off the black sheet and hood, and threw them into his bag. He had counted on the council being so stunned at his appearance that it would take them a minute to react, and fortunately, he was right. The whole council was so surprised that they froze in place. The chief of police was standing there with his mouth open. So shocked were they that no one moved for almost a minute, then they all moved at once, bumping and knocking each other over.

The council was yelling and banging against the door trying to get out. The pressure broke the handles, and the doors flew open, almost knocking Oceans down.

"Get the hell out of the way, boy!" the police chief roared.

The council was in mass confusion. After he regained his balance, Oceans went on out of the door and walked away, congratulating himself on pulling this fool stunt off yet berating himself for taking such a risk.

Unable to find Black Sheet, the committee returned to the council chambers. Seats were overturned, water glasses were broken, papers were scattered, and nerves were stretched taut.

"Of all the goddamn nerve!" Mayor Simmons cursed.

"Why didn't you grab him, chief?" the district attorney complained.

"It happened so fast. I was too shocked to move. Anyway, I never saw him."

"Everybody was to stunned to move," another council member conceded.

The unexpected visit of Black Sheet to the council meeting resulted in them ending in confusion and accomplishing nothing.

COLORED VFW CLUB AND MEETING WITH WILLIE HORTON

As a recent army veteran, Oceans's first visit to the colored VFW club was special for two reasons. He had watched his father—an army veteran—go off to the club as a young boy, and now he too had earned that right and could speak on the same level with the other veterans. Also, he could bond with his father on a different level.

"I've always wanted to come here with you, Dad, because you always seemed so happy and loose when you came home."

"Well, a man's got to have a little recreation to keep him sane, son."

They had their first beer together, and he felt closer to his father than he ever had.

"I'm still worried about this Black Sheet thing, son."

"I know, and I don't want you to worry. I've got some of those undercover Klan members thinking twice before they put on the sheet."

Before they could discuss Black Sheet further, Willie Horton—a friend of his father's walked up.

"Hey, Willie, things must be going pretty good for you to be away from your farm this time of day."

"Well, I had a good year. Now if I can just get Mr. Tuckee to see it that way, I'll be fine."

"Still cheating his sharecroppers, huh?"

"Yeah, his figures always show a loss, but I've got my own figures this year, and I know I made a profit. I kept track of everything I bought and spent and the dates. If his figures are different, I'm going to show him mine. You're good at figures, ain't you, Enoch?"

"Yeah, I've been doing my own books for years. Oh, excuse my manners. You remember my son Oceans?"

"I swear I wouldn't have known him if I'd met him on the street. Good to see you, Oceans. Enoch, I need somebody to double-check my calculations before I present them to Tuckee."

"Let me see what you got."

After carefully checking the math, Enoch and Oceans only found a couple of minor mistakes before giving it their approval.

"Thanks, Enoch, Oceans. If he sees one thing wrong, he'll say it's all wrong."

"How's he going to take this?"

"He ain't going to like it, but I don't give a damn."

"Will you put your sharecrop in jeopardy?"

"I'm his best producer, and I know he's overextended and needs every penny he can get. I don't see him cutting his own throat. But it's a chance I have to take. This year, I'm making a stand. Maybe this Black Sheet thing gave me courage—I don't know."

THE PLANTER SOCIETY

Planters were at the top of Caloosa society. They had a free hand to run their property as they saw fit, and no one was allowed to question their methods. Whatever the planter said was law, and there was no possibility of appeal or alleviating the situation. The planters' verdict was final. They controlled the prosperity of the sharecroppers that worked their land. Some were very generous and allowed sharecroppers to make a little annual profit after crops and expenses were considered. But most ran their property like labor camps and kept their sharecroppers in perpetual debt, never allowing them to show a profit even if they made one. Some of the sharecroppers never saw any money year after year.

One of the worst of the planters and most prolific and unscrupulous swindlers was Tuckee Brookstone. He was notorious for cheating and mistreating his workers, showing them no grace and no mercy. His hate for colored folks was so great that the hate and hostility of other whites in Caloosa paled in its intensity when compared to his hatred. Over the years, Brookstone's family had maintained the former slave quarters left from the days of slavery on the Brookstone Plantation where he held all of his meetings with his colored sharecroppers. Although slavery had been abolished over eighty years, he liked to remind his colored sharecroppers that they still weren't far from slavery. He still ran his property in the image of the old slavery days. He was absolute ruler, his word was final, and he tolerated no back talk.

He kept his sharecroppers in debt so that they couldn't go anywhere else. He maintained the books of their production and purchases, and they weren't allowed to question his bookkeeping. His sharecroppers were the lowest compensated workers in the region, and they couldn't leave unless their debts were paid in full under the threat of prison.

None of the planters were overly generous, but many of them allowed their sharecroppers to show a little profit at the end of the season if they worked hard and produced a good profitable crop. But none of Brookstone's sharecroppers had seen any actual money in years. With no cash to spend, they were forced to charge their clothing, tools, food, and anything else that they couldn't make or grow at the company store at outrageous prices.

Brookstone did all of the bookkeeping and forbade them to question his figures. Every year, he called the sharecroppers up to the former slave overseer's house, which he had maintained and used as an office. Another reminder of their status in his eyes. One by one, he called them in to go over the books with them and tell them what they owed. If the sharecropper had a particularly desirable wife, he would suggest that he could lower the debt a little if they sent their wife up to his house for the night. No one had taken him up on that proposition so far.

WILLIE STOOD HIS GROUND

Willie stood back and looked at his work with pride. "This is our best year yet. We doubled our production," he told his wife, Dorothy. "If this was our land, we would prosper."

Willie Horton was a young sharecropper on Tuckee's land. In the five years since Willie and his family had taken over the farm, he had always ended the year in debt no matter how big the harvest was or how hard he and his wife worked.

This year, Willie had done his own bookkeeping, itemizing everything he had charged and keeping track of his productivity and the current prices buyers were paying. Then he had double-checked his figures with trusted friends at the VFW club. Now he was ready to confront Brookstone. He planned to compare his figures to Brookstone's numbers, and if Brookstone didn't like it, he could take his farm and stick it, and Willie would take his family and move on. He figured with his production, Brookstone had more to lose than to gain by letting him go. In fact, according to his figures, he had made enough to pay off all of his debts and have a few dollars left in his pocket. That's what he intended to tell Brookstone.

His wife, Dorothy, was afraid for him. She knew he had a temper and, if he thought he was right, he would never give in. He would go to any length.

"Honey," she said before he went to the meeting with Mr. Brookstone, "if he won't listen to you, just let it go. Don't push. Getting yourself lynched won't help us."

"I've got good records, and I can back up my claim. It won't get no better if I just let it go."

He was a good farmer and an asset to any planter, and everyone knew it. In fact he had been called exceptional. His crops were requested by buyers. Two years ago, he had been offered another farm by one of Mr. Brookstone's competitors, but he couldn't take it because he was in debt to Brookstone and had to turn it down, and yet Mr. Brookstone still cheated him.

He kept silent as Brookstone went over his figures with him. Every year, he was charged for items he never used. This year, he was charged for a new plow, whiskey, tobacco, and even borrowing some money. That Brookstone was cheating him was plain, and he didn't care if he knew.

"You did pretty good," Brookstone complimented him, "but you can do better."

The farmers standing outside waiting were speechless. They had never heard Brookstone compliment a colored man before, and he seemed to mean it.

"You can do better too, Mr. Brookstone," Willie replied.

"Wh-what did you say?"

"I said you can do better too, Brookstone."

"Of all the—you better explain, and it better be good." No colored man had ever talked to him like that before, and it caught him by surprise, left him at a loss for words. Finally, all he could think to say was, "What do you mean by that, Willie?"

"What I mean," he said, raising his voice unintentionally and emphasizing his point, "is that your bookkeeping is wrong."

"What!" "You dare, huh? Huh, of all the nerve, huh—" He lost his voice again. His lips were moving, but no sound was coming out.

The men waiting outside suddenly got quiet. They wanted to hear every word. Willie was doing something they all wanted to do, but none had the nerve or could afford to do. Their livelihood was tied up in their sharecrop. Even if it wasn't much, they needed it to support their families. Every year, they grew deeper and deeper in debt with no hope of repaying. They were at the mercy of Brookstone's greed, and it had no compassion. They listened as Willie challenged Tuckee Brookstone's bookkeeping. He was speaking for all of them.

Before Brookstone could get his thoughts together again, Willie continued to reprimand him. "I never bought a new plow, and I don't smoke or drink whiskey, and you know it, and you know I didn't borrow any money on account. You're the one with the nerve," he told Brookstone. "You got me mixed up with somebody else."

"Are you calling me a liar, Willie?" Brookstone asked, his voice going up in anger.

"Damn right I am, Mr. Brookstone. You're lying through your teeth, and I'm not going to take it anymore. I can read and I can count, and I kept this list of everything I bought from your store, and I didn't buy no plow, no whiskey, no tobacco, and no money."

"I say you did, so you are calling me a liar and a cheat to boot. Is that right, Willie?" Brookstone repeated in his most menacing voice, trying to intimidate him.

He didn't say anything for a minute, then Willie looked him in the eyes and said, "That's right, Tuckee. You a lie and a cheat, and this ain't the first time. You do it every year. You've cheated me out of enough money to buy this damn farm."

"You dare to look me in the eye, call me by my first name, and call me a lie and a cheat? Don't let this Black Sheet stuff go to your head."

"This ain't got nothing to do with Black Sheet. You just a lie and a cheat," Willie repeated with intensity. "That's just what you is, Tuckee."

"You uppity-ass nigger, I'll whip you to within an inch of your life!" Tuckee screamed, reaching for a nearby whip.

Willie still stood his ground. "Don't do it, Tuckee. I ain't taking no whippin' from you."

Mr. Brookstone, certain that Willie was bluffing in spite of his determined look and stance, lifted the whip and started his swing. Willie stepped in with a powerful right that broke Brookstone's nose. He then took the whip, lashed Blackstone across the back a couple of times and threw it out the door, reached down, and grabbed Brookstone by the collar. The look in Brookstone's eyes was one of terror.

"Don't ever try that again," he said. "Now give me credit for what I did and mark me paid in full. I know how much money I made."

"I'll get you for this!" Brookstone yelled.

WILLIE'S AFTERMATH

He was still too mad to think about what he had done and what it might mean. One thing was sure. They had to find a place to stay. Dorothy, his wife, was waiting at the door with a worried look when he arrived home.

"How did he take it when you showed him your books?"

"He tried to hit me with a whip."

"Oh my Lord, what did you do?"

"I walked out." He didn't tell her what he did before he walked out.

"So you still haven't settled anything?"

He couldn't think of the right words to tell her then, so he just said no. He figured she'd know soon enough when the police or the KKK came for him. He had stood up for his rights, and he wasn't going to run.

Brookstone had immediately sent the other sharecroppers home and called the grand dragon.

"I need a meeting ASAP," Tuckee Brookstone said over the phone. It was a party line so he couldn't say much more to his friend the mayor. "Those niggers are crazy as a betsey bug if they think I'm gonna let them get away with this." He smiled to himself. Maybe a little visit from the KKK will set them straight. "I've got a sharecropper that's giving me a problem and making the other share croppers rebel. I need to teach him a lesson. Maybe the Klan can teach him some manners."

"Have you forgotten that this is a party line?"

"I don't care."

"Why don't I come out there, and we'll talk about it."

"Okay, but as soon as possible, this can't wait."

While he waited for the mayor/ grand dragon to come, Brookstone tried to think of something he could do to Willie to save the face he lost in front of the other sharecroppers. He had to do something, or they would all rebel.

The other sharecroppers walked away, still reeling from the scene they had just witnessed. They admired Willie for his courage, but they were afraid for him. Brookstone couldn't let this go. He had to save face. He had cheated all of his sharecroppers, both colored and white, although the white tenant farmers were allowed to show some profit.

Suddenly Garrett, Willie's closest neighbor, stopped and faced the other farmers. "I'm thinking it's time for all of us to stick together and get behind Willie. He started something that can help all of us, and think about it. Willie said Brookstone just brought a bunch of new equipment. He's more in debt than we are."

"That's right," another farmer joined in. "He can't get rid of all of us. We all been thinking we needed him, but he needs us. Without us, he loses everything."

"I don't know about this," Felton, who never showed much backbone and was doubtful of everything, declared, shaking his head. "This ain't our problem. Why should we stick our necks out? Willie brought this on hisself."

"I tell you what," another farmer suggested. "Why don't we think about this until tomorrow?"

"Tomorrow is too late," Garrett said. "Now is the time. Let's go back and face him now. Let him know all of us are behind Willie, and we want fair treatment. We all made a profit this year, and we want to see it on the books. Come on," he urged, turning back toward Brookstone.

"I told you boys to go home!" Brookstone yelled angrily when he saw them coming back. "I'll let you know when I want to see you. Now get."

"First, there's no boys here." Garrett was mad now, very mad. "Second, we want to see you now."

Brookstone turned red as a beet. He started to say something, but the words wouldn't come out. He'd never faced a rebellion before.

"Third, we stand behind Willie. We're tired of being cheated, and we want it to end now. We all made a profit this year, and we want to see it on the books, and we want to see our debts go down too. Fourth, if Willie goes, we go too."

"You all owe me money. The only place you're going is to jail!"

"I told y—" Felton started to say.

"Shut up!" Garrett cut him off. "Believe me, Tuckee, if we stay and don't get what we want, it'll be worse for you than for us. Can you afford to lose the income from eight farms?"

"Can you afford to lose your life?" Tuckee said, walking away.

"You gonna kill us all!" Garrett yelled to his back.

"I told ya! I told ya!" Felton cried. "Now look what you've done."

"So what's this all about, Tuckee?" the grand dragon asked, sipping a beer at the planters' private club.

"I want to lynch a nigger."

"Nothing like getting right to the point, huh, Tuckee?"

"I don't have time to beat around the bush."

The busboy, who was a seventy-year-old black man, was cleaning off the table next to theirs, but they just ignored him and kept right on talking. He was no threat to them. After all, what was he going to do?

"So what happened?"

"It's Willie Horton. He—"

"Wait, Willie Horton? I thought he was your best producer."

"He was, but now he's got the other farmers all stirred up, planting stories in their heads about being cheated and overcharged, and now they're rebelling. I need to make an example out of him."

"Well, aren't you?" the grand dragon said, laughing.

"Aren't I what?"

"Aren't you cheating them?"

"Come on, this is no joke. It's serious. A big producer don't mean nothing if they're causing problems." He went on to tell his friend what happened, and the busboy heard most of it. They either didn't notice or didn't care that the busboy took so long cleaning off one table.

"I've got them all coming up to the big house day after tomorrow. They think they're going to get bonuses and get out of debt, but I've got a surprise for them."

"I'll see what I can do about a little surprise party," the grand dragon promised.

ROSCOE AT REDS

Reds was like a barbershop. That's where you learned all the gossip and a lot of the facts too if you wanted a drink instead of a haircut. The more they drank, the more they talked, and in his short time back, Oceans had learned that this was the place to go to pick up on the latest news.

That's where he was when Roscoe, the busboy, downed his first shot of gin and told everybody of Brookstone's plans for Willie Horton.

"Too bad they killed that Black Sheep fellow. Horton's gonna need him for sure and some of those other farmers too."

"Don't you read the papers? Black Sheep is not dead."

"Are you sure about this, Roscoe?" Oceans asked.

"I was standing right there. They didn't try to hide it, acted just like I was deaf and dumb."

"You have to admit, Roscoe," one of the bystanders observed, "you do qualify for that last part."

"Screw you, Percy." Everybody laughed.

"See you guys later," Oceans said, rushing to the door.

"Where you going in such a hurry? Ain't nothing you can do about it. We can't stop it."

"There's one thing I can do," Oceans said, stopping for a moment.

"What's that?"

"I can warn him," he answered, going through the door.

The next day, the grand dragon make a special trip to see Tuckee, but he had bad news.

"Sorry, Tuckee, nobody is willing to put on the sheets until Black Sheep is caught and killed."

"The hell you say. The Klan's been terrorizing niggers for almost one hundred years, and you mean one lone man done terrorized them?"

"One unknown dangerous man who has shot up the houses of some of our most prominent covert members and threatened to shoot them up again. They're afraid for their families. His anonymity, knowledge of our membership, and threats have unnerved everybody. You're just going to have to live with this for a while."

Tuckee looked down and just shook his head. He couldn't suppress his feeling of anger and disgust. For the first time, the Klan was letting him down. They were actually so intimidated by Black Sheep that they wouldn't even show themselves for the cause that they were created for—keep the niggers in line.

This news was forcing him to change his plans and his attitude. His whole financial future was at stake if his crops failed. Even though it hurt like hell, he called his sharecroppers together and said that because of their years of dedication, he was willing to take another look at his books—at that point, he almost bit his tongue off. "And you come back tomorrow. Maybe I did make a mistake somewhere."

"Ain't no maybe to it," Felton said, defiantly speaking for the first time. "Oh, and, Mr. Brookstone, we don't like meeting at this slave overseer's cabin. We'll come up to the house."

"Felton!" Garrett said, surprised.

That got Brookstone's attention, and about the same time, the sheriff drove up. He saw all of the colored sharecroppers standing around and immediately asked, "Are you having a problem with these boys, Tuckee?"

"Come on up to the office, sheriff. We need to talk. What's happening with you and the rest of the Klan? Is it really true that this Black Sheet character has scared the dog shit out of all of you. You know I always thought you all were only brave running in a pack with your faces covered. Without those white sheets, hoods, and the rest of the pack, the Klan is just a bunch of cowards."

"I can't believe you're saying that after all we've done to keep the niggers in their place. I'll see you later, Tuckee, and I'll expect an apology."

"Okay, Willie, what's going on?"
"Nothing, Dorothy."
"Why are you so quiet?"
"Who me?"
"Yeah, you. Who else would I be talking to?"
"I was just thinking."
"About what?"
"Nothing much."
"I've been married to you long enough to know something's wrong. What did your hot temper get you into now? I'll bet it's something about those books. What did you do, Willie? You didn't tell me the truth, did you?"

"I hit Mr. Brookstone." He said it so low that she didn't think she heard him right.

"You did what?"

"Hit Mr. Brookstone."

"Oh my god, Willie, you didn't."

"Well, he tried to whip me, and I don't take that from no man, black or white. I'll die first."

"What are we going to do? You know they coming for you."

"If they come, maybe that Black Sheet we been hearing about will show up. He helped Steve and Bobby Sweeten. Maybe he'll help us."

"You can't depend on that, Willie. We've got to run. I don't want to lose you."

"I'm not running, Dorothy. I'm sorry. I'm not running. I took as much as I could."

"Okay, Willie, whatever happens, I'll stand by you. I'm proud of you for standing up for yourself. Now come on in. I've got some coffee on. We'll face this together."

"Hey, Willie, are you in there?"

"That sounds like Garrett."

"Was he there?"

"Everybody was. Come on, may as well see what he wants.

"Hey Garrett, what are all of you doing here? I was expecting the police or the KKK."

"Sorry. They're not coming."

"They'll be coming all right because Brookstone can't afford to let me get away with humiliating him and hitting him. He needs his farmers to stay in their place and be submissive. That's not me anymore."

"Brookstone's not sending anybody after you because we told him that if you go, we all go. Anyway, I heard Wesley Simmons tell him that the Klan ain't coming—they're afraid of that Black Sheet fellow."

"This ain't no joke, Garrett. Stop playing around, and get out of here before you all get in trouble. You've got families to feed."

"We figure what you did can help us all. You're not the only one being cheated and kept in debt. And we're not the only ones in debt. Brookstone is in debt up to his eyeballs, and he can't afford for us to leave or slow down. We've got him by the balls. He's going to redo the books, and he wants us all at his house tomorrow. He said to bring you too. We're meeting at the back of his house, not the overseer's cabin, and guess who spoke up and said we not meeting at the overseer's cabin anymore? Get ready to faint. It was Felton."

"I know I'm dreaming now."

"Before we go to the house, we're going to make sure that we never meet at the overseer's cabin again."

"How we gonna do that?"

"We gonna have a barn fire, hah, make that a cabin fire—a overseer's cabin! Ha ha ha!"

"Leave it to God because God can," Dorothy whispered.

"I'll believe it when I see it," Willie declared.

"If it happens, it'll be the second miracle in two days."

"What was the first miracle?"

"We stood up together. He would have killed me by myself."

Then Willie did something he had never done or even thought about doing. He hugged them all one at a time.

Dorothy Horton sat in the window and listened to the men talking, celebrating, and drinking moonshine. Again, she said to herself, *I'll never understand men. Do they really think Mr. Brookstone is going to let them get away with this?*

The next day after Willie had sobered up, Dorothy sat him down and brought up the subject of Mr. Brookstone. "Willie, I know how proud you are of your friends for standing with you, but now in the light of day, do you really think Mr. Brookstone is going to let this stand?"

He was silent for a minute then said, "According to Garrett, he seemed pretty sincere. Said he was going to go back over his books then call everybody up to the big house and settle up."

"Settle up how? Maybe it won't be the way you think. Don't trust him, honey."

"We got to."

Later on that same day, Willie called the other farmers together.

"I was just thinking," he started off. "Maybe we shouldn't trust Brookstone. Maybe he's got something else planned for our meeting."

"Like what?" Garrett asked. "We've got him over a barrow. He's deep in debt. The Klan ain't coming. He can't do nothing. He needs us as much as we need him. You're making something out of nothing."

"Well, it won't hurt to think about it and be ready for foul play. I'm just saying we should be prepared for anything. Don't trust him."

MEETING AT THE BIG HOUSE
WHERE DEMANDS ARE MADE

Willie decided to not let his wife's doubts deter him from his secret plan to go all out in his demands from Mr. Brookstone.

"After rechecking my books, I've found some areas where I can make some concessions. Is something burning? I smell smoke."

Felton sniffed the air. "I don't smell anything, Mr. Brookstone."

"It's nothing. What were you saying?"

"As I was saying, for the most part, my books are correct, but because of your loyalty, I've made a special effort to make sure that all of you make a few dollars profit this season. As to your figures, Willie, I'm not in complete agreement with them, but I will take off the charge for all of the items that you disputed, thereby giving you a real nice profit. I hope that satisfies everyone's concerns.

"I knew something was burning. I can see the smoke. It's the overseer's cabin! It's on fire! Reggie, Damn you. I told you to be careful with those matches."

"Let's see if we can put it out," Willie said, getting up.

"It's too late," Tuckee retorted with a frown. Aggravation was evident in his voice. "Let's finish this up."

Willie's fellow farmers were so ecstatic that they didn't even notice his displeasure. For the first time ever, they had made a profit and would actually have a few dollars in their pockets.

"Was there something else, Willie?"

"Yes, sir. Been with you over ten years, and this is the first time since I started that I've been out of debt to you. I've decided that this is a good time to relocate. I'm giving up my sharecrop and moving on."

This decision was like a financial death blow to Tuckee. Willie was his best producer farming on his best land, and he desperately needed his production this season just to keep his head above water and next season to break even. Now his problem was how to get him to stay without revealing his dire situation.

He cleared his throat and looked around at the others before responding. They were in shock. He had surprised everyone. "If everyone else is satisfied, you can go, and Willie and I will work this out."

"We'll just wait here with Willie until he's ready to leave," Garrett responded, afraid Tuckee would try something underhanded.

"That's okay, Garrett. You all go on. Don't worry—I'll be fine."

When they were alone, Tuckee asked, "What brought this on? I've accepted your demands, and you're still dissatisfied."

"I may never get this chance again. Since I'm out of debt and don't have to worry about going to jail if I leave, I'm going."

"What would it take to persuade you to stay?"

"I would have to know that me and my family would never be in debt to you again."

"You have something in mind, Willie. What is it?"

"You have seventy-five acres of land south of my sharecrop. If you sigh it over to me, I can put in a small crop of my own and wouldn't have to go into debt to you again."

Tuckee didn't hesitate. He was furious. "Nigger, are you crazy? Get the hell away from my house! I ought to have you killed for trying to blackmail me into giving you land. Get off my farm!"

Oceans heard—to his surprise—that Willie had won his dispute against Tuckee Brookstone, and all of the farmers had been compensated with their first profits ever. But then Willie had informed him that he was giving up the farm and going north. It was anybody's guess what would happen now.

Tuckee thought long and hard about the proposition Willie had offered. That seventy-five acres wasn't putting a penny into his pocket, and he couldn't find anyone to sharecrop on it because so many black farmers were migrating north thanks to that damn black *Defender* newspaper. If he gave Willy the seventy-five acres and took 50 percent of the profit for, say, ten years, he couldn't lose. He'd have to talk to Willie first thing in the morning.

First thing the next day, he did something he had never done before. He went to Willie's house instead of sending for him. His arrival caught Willie and his wife by surprise and created near panic, but Willie was determined to maintain his composure no matter what the visit was about.

"Can we talk in private for a moment?" Tuckee asked. Before Willie could say anything, again catching Willie by surprise and himself too—this was completely out of character for a plantation owner speaking to a black sharecropper—he continued, "First, I acted rather hastily and thoughtlessly in ordering you off the plantation when you asked me about the seventy-five acres that I'm not using. After giving it some thought, I think I can let you have it for, say, 50 percent of the profit for ten years at which time the seventy-five acres would become yours."

Willie thought for a few seconds before answering, "Mr. Tuckee, I sho do appreciate you thinking about this, and I've thought about it too. I was thinking more in the line of 20 percent for two years. I'm going to load those fields up with more crops that even you would think impossible, and you'll make a bundle of money from your portion. I'll stay and take it for 20 percent for two years."

"I gave you my price, and I'm not obliged to change it."

"I'm sorry to hear that, sir, because I want to come to an agreement, but I just can't do it for that. The seventy-five acres don't mean that much to me. I'll get my family off your place as soon as I can pick this crop for you."

Brookstone looked at Willie for a moment before answering. *I didn't think this nigger was this smart,* he thought to himself then said, "I wouldn't usually do this, Willie, but I like your guts and you're a hard worker. I'll go 35 percent for six years."

"Make it 25 percent for three years, and we got a deal, Mr. Brookstone."

Tuckee just looked at him for a minute then said, "Okay, I'll accept that."

"When can we put it in writing, sir?"

As he walked away, Tuckee said to himself, *The nerve of that nigger. If I wasn't in such bad shape financially*—he couldn't finish.

LYNCHING THE GRAND DRAGON

After his whole KKK chapter had refused to go out and lynch Willie Horton, Wesley Simmons, mayor and grand dragon of the Klu Klux Klan, called an emergency meeting at the courthouse—the KKK meeting hall had been destroyed by Black Sheet.

He got right to the point. "What do you mean you're not going out until Black Sheet is caught and lynched?"

Elden Green, one of the first Klansmen to be terrorized by Black Sheet, stood up to answer. "It's just like we said, too dangerous with this Black Sheet character running loose. I've already lost one truck and barely got away with my life. If I lose that, I can't replace it. Now he's shooting up homes and putting families in danger. He seems to know who all of our members are. For all I know," he cautioned, looking around suspiciously, "he may be sitting here right now. Until he's caught or identified, I'm not going on any more raids."

"What do I have here—a bunch of cowards without the courage to meet the obligations required as Knights of the Ku Klux Klan? You signed an oath. Did you forget?"

"The oath didn't say anything about getting shot at or killed or losing your property or having your family terrorized. We're supposed to do the terrorizing, and that's what I signed up for—to terrorize, intimidate, and spread fear among the blacks, not to be terrorized," Andrew Bonaparte stressed.

"Me too!" echoed around the room.

"I joined up to kill niggers, not to get killed."

"So at the first sign of trouble, you're backing out?"

"Not backing out, using good judgment."

"We can't let these niggers think they can defy us and get away with it. We've got to pay this Willie a visit and teach him a lesson, or the rest of them will get out of hand."

"What do you mean we? When is the last time you went on a night raid? While we're out there being shot at and shot up, you're at home safe and sound."

"I'm going on this one, but first, I've got to run out to my farm and take care of some business."

The colored courthouse janitor whom they regarded as of no consequence was in the hall listening to every word. To them, he was just part of the woodwork.

Oceans had made it a practice of stopping by Red's to see what information he could pick up that might help Black Sheet prevent another black lynching. He had learned from experience that all you had to do was listen. Everybody had a white-folks story. He could get all kinds of information just by keeping his ears open. After a few drinks, they would unwind and vent their frustrations and gossip about the information picked up at work. Some of it was pretty good.

Whites were notorious for talking freely about anything with their colored employees in the room. They were so naïve that they didn't see colored employees as a threat. In fact, like the air, colored folks became invisible in the presence of whites, so that many times colored folks knew what was coming before it was even carried out.

This trip to Red's paid off sooner than he expected. He had barely touched his beer when Austin Grant, the courthouse janitor, came in and started talking about how Black Sheet had scared the hell out of the KKK. The grand dragon wanted them to raid Willy Horton's house and teach him a lesson, but Black Sheet got them so scared they won't do it.

"Wesley Simmon say he gonna lead them soon as he come back from his farm. Dis I gotta see. Somebody better tell Willie."

"Why don't you tell him?"

"Not me. I'm staying out of dis here stuff."

"Hey, Austin, when is he going to his farm?" Oceans asked.

"Said he was goin' tomorrow afternoon. He's been trying to sell it, and he's meeting a buyer out there."

Oceans left the bar and drove out to the grand dragon's farm to look around.

The next day when the grand dragon got to his farm, Black Sheet was there waiting. After looking in the barn, house, and yard without finding the buyer, the grand dragon started to curse and talk aloud to himself. He yelled into the air, "Where the hell are you? I don't have all day! Damn it! I told that real estate idiot I wouldn't have much time!"

"He's not here, but Black Sheet is," a voice exploded out of the silence like a gunshot and reverberated in his ear.

Black Sheet! Black Sheet?

A man in a black sheet and hood stepped out about fifty yards away holding a rifle pointed right at his chest. "I paid somebody to tell your man to meet you at the feed store in town, and I came out here to wait for you."

"You hypocrite! What do you want? Nobody is being lynched out here!"

"Not yet anyway."

"What does that mean? How the hell did you know I would be out here anyhow?" he asked, trying get a better look the person who was talking. "You told us at the meeting. Don't you remember?"

"You! You were at the meeting?"

"I never miss a meeting, Wesley."

"And don't call me Wesley."

"That's your name, ain't it? At least, that's what we call you at the meetings."

"What's in this for you? Why are you doing this?"

"Did you know the Negroes were emancipated during the Civil War back in 1863?"

"Now you even sound like one of them. Okay, what do you want?"

"I want the Klan to stop terrorizing and lynching colored people."

"Look, Black Sheet or whatever your name is, you don't understand. If we don't keep them in their place, pretty soon they'll start to think they're equal."

"Well, aren't they?"

"We're white. Black people are just naturally inferior to us, and we have to keep reminding them. We're going to keep terrorizing and lynching them as long as they try to be equal. First thing you know, they'll want to vote, share our schools, sit at our lunch counters, and marry our women."

"So you think lynching is the answer to teaching them a lesson? Well, in that case, I think you should know how it feels to be lynched."

"How the hell am I going to know that?"

"It's simple—I'll give you a demonstration. I'm going to lynch you."

"Lynch me? You're crazy! You can't lynch a white man!"

"Watch me. Any man can be lynched. Lynching has nothing to do with color. All it takes is that the lyncher is inhumane, savage, ruthless, sadistic, and very brutal—and right now, I'm overflowing with all of those traits. But I have some compassion. I'm not going to lynch you unless I'm wearing the right attire," he said, throwing a white sheet around himself. "Very soon now, you'll know how a black man feels when a bunch of cowardly white men hiding behind a white sheets and hoods are preparing to lynch him."

Black Sheet had already stacked some logs, and he started pouring kerosene on them.

"Don't be ridiculous. You can't lynch me. I'm a grand dragon."

"Still arrogant, huh? Being a pompous asshole right to the end, huh?" Black Sheet went over and tied him up amidst the curses and resistance. "Now we're going to play a game. We'll pretend you're no longer a grand dragon nor a Klansman. In fact, not even a white man. For the purpose of this little amusement, you're a black man whose been accused of breaking a Jim Crow law, and you've got to be taught a lesson. I'm going to pretend to be the Klan coming to lynch you. You really haven't done anything, but you're going to be lynched anyway just 'cause you're black. You're scared, terrified, and helpless."

As Black Sheet said that, he kicked Wesley in the stomach, then again in the kidney, then a vicious kick between the legs, and Wesley started yelling and crying and begging then peed and messed on himself. Now he really believed that Black Sheet was really going to lynch him. "Okay, this joke has gone far enough."

"You think this is a joke. I'll bet no black man ever thought it was a joke. You're being called foul names, teased, laughed at, whipped, poked with a hot poker, branded, cut, belittled and dehumanized, brutalized, bastardized, degraded, demoralized. Nobody comes to your aid because you're only a black man. You're expendable. You start to whimper, scream, cry, and, dead man, you know it."

"You can't do this. It's not human!" Wesley Simmons pleaded.

"I'm giving you a chance to see how it feels to be lynched. It's different when the shoe is on the other foot, ain't it?"

"Noooo! Please don't," the grand dragon pleaded. "I'm sorry."

"But this is what you like to do to colored people. Now you know how it feels."

"You can't. I'm a white man like you."

"Not like me. Now I'll douse you with kerosene so I can set you on fire."

"No! No! Please. Don't burn me."

"Remember Osie Obiri? You set him on fire and watched him burn."

"I'm sorry. I'm sorry."

"Sorry won't bring my friend back."

"Your friend?"

Black Sheet snatched his hood off and let the grand dragon see that he was black.

"You're black? You're black!"

"Now we'll pull your pants down and cut off your genitals."

"No! No! Not that." He was getting hysterical, peeing again.

"Then pierce your skin with hot pokers." Black Sheet touched his skin lightly with a hot poker.

"You can't do that. That's barbaric, primitive, and uncivilized."

"Too bad you didn't think of that when you were doing the lynching."

The grand dragon saw the look in his eyes, and now that he had seen his face, he knew he was doomed. Black Sheet struck a match.

"Please. Don't set me on fire. Don't you see I'm a white man? You can't lynch a white man. No, you can't lynch a white man. It's just not done."

"Firsthand experience is the best teacher. I'm doing it for you. Now I'll douse you with kerosene so I can set you on fire."

Black Sheet then poured some more kerosene over his clothes.

The grand dragon started screaming, "Don't set me on fire! Don't set me on fire! I'm a white man! You can't lynch a white man! You're a black man. You're supposed to have compassion for your white masters."

When Wesley Simmons didn't come home that night, his wife called the sheriff to see if they had seen him. No one had seen him, but the sheriff told her not to worry—they would look around. It crossed their minds that maybe Black Sheet had got him.

Early the next morning, a white man wearing Klan paraphernalia was found lynched and hanging from a tree on Main Street. It was the same tree that a black man had been hanged from a few weeks earlier. The body was identified as that of Wesley Simmons.

The scene of Wesley Simmons lynching soon became a spectacle. No one had even seen or heard of a member of the Klan being lynched before. Spectators were coming from miles around to witness this phenomenon. The Klan in Caloosa was in a state of shock and panic. Widespread fear engulfed them. Some of the closet members of the Klan became hysterical, even burning anything that identified them with the Klan. They feared what Black Sheet would do next.

The Klan ceased to operate in Caloosa, and the colored population, especially the men, could rest easy.

ACKNOWLEDGMENTS

Thanks to the authors of these books which I found informative
While writing this book of fiction

FORGOTTEN
Linda Hervieux

THE WARMTH OF OTHER SUNS
Isabel Wilkerson

THE FALL OF THE ASANTE EMPIRE
Robert B. G. Edgerton

IN THEIR OWN WORDS
Edited by Milton Meltzer

THE CHITLIN CIRCUIT: AND THE ROAD TO ROCK 'N ROLL
Preston Lauterrach

CPSIA information can be obtained
at www.ICGtesting.com
Printed in the USA
BVHW070954080419
544914BV00009B/204/P